Kernowland

Invasion of Evil

Book Three

Titles available in the Kernowland series:

Kernowland 1 The Crystal Pool
Kernowland 2 Darkness Day
Kernowland 3 Invasion of Evil

To St Martin's School

Kernowland

Invasion of Evil

Jack Trelawny

CAMPION BOOKS

A catalogue record for this book
is available from the British Library

ISBN 978-0-9546338-6-8

Campion Books is an Imprint of Campion Publishing Limited

Illustrations by Louise Hackman-Hexter

Printed and bound in Great Britain by
William Clowes Ltd., Beccles, Suffolk

First published in the UK in 2007 by

CAMPION BOOKS
2 Lea Valley House
Stoney Bridge Drive
Waltham Abbey
Essex, UK
EN9 3LY

www.kernowland.com

For Tizzie and Louis

AUTHOR'S NOTES

Apart from Tizzie & Louis,
the characters and events in this book
are entirely fictitious.

Any similarity to real events or actual persons,
living or dead, would be extremely worrying.

In this book,
'Erth' means 'Earth',
and 'Wurld' means 'World'.

Website
There is lots of other information
on the Kernowland website

www.kernowland.com

ONE

PIRANHASHARKS!

'PIRANHASHARKS!' shouted Squint for the second time.

'Help me!' gurgled Tizzie, as she bobbed up from under the waves once more.

The desperate girl gasped a breath, then screamed in terror as a thousand black dorsal fins cut through the swirling sea towards her.

'HELLLLLLLLLLLLP MEEEEEE!'

The water foamed and frothed and fizzed as the thrashing, threshing, bubbling, burbling sound got louder and louder.

The shoalpack moved as one giant Chewing Creature.

And the creature was ravenous!

TWO

Desert Riders

Louis emerged on the other side of the Crystal Door.

But something was wrong.

A vast desert of sand dunes stretched out before him.

He obviously wasn't in Jungleland.

A gusting wind whirled across the dunes, whipping up the sand so that it stung his eyes and got in his nose and mouth.

Where am I? he asked himself, as he covered his face with his hands. Did I say the wrong words before I stepped into the Crystal Door?

Then Louis started to tremble.

Looking between his fingers through the dusty haze, he could just make out about a dozen men riding on camels along the top of a dune in the near-distance.

The men were all dressed from head-to-toe in sand-coloured robes, with material covering their faces, apart from a slit for their eyes.

Louis had no way of knowing whether these desert riders were friend or foe.

He tried to think fast.

Should I use the Golden Key to go back? But what if the people who killed the King and Queen and Mr Sand are waiting for me in the Golden Cavern? Shall I run? But where? There's only sand in every direction.

Louis squinted.

As he focused his gaze, he saw the camelmen notice him.

They drew their scimitars and whipped their steeds into a gallop.

'Wooooowoowooowoowoooooooo!'

The desert riders were now heading straight towards the frightened young boy, waving their curved swords and shrieking wildly.

'Wooooowoowooowoowoooooooo!'

One of them was aiming a musket straight at him.

Louis began to panic.

THREE

Dribble's End

'He's for it now, Spikey, oh yes he is.'

Melanchol Drym continued to shout dementedly and wave his sharp heavy stick wildly above his head as he stood over little Dribble, who shivered with fear and whimpered submissively.

Wendron, now beside the disgusting dustman, pointed Whackit, her rulerwand, at the little dust-dog.

'Let me see. Yes, I'll put an Exploding Spell on him.'

'Oh no… noohhh. Please, Miss Wendron. Can't Spikey and I finish him? Please. It's only fair. Oh yes it is. Please, Miss Wendron. Let us do it. We'll do it properly. Slowly. Oh yes we will. Pleeease.'

'Oh, go on then,' said Wendron, with quite a bit of disappointment in her voice… she hadn't exploded anyone for months.

'Oh thank you, Miss Wendron, thank you,' fawned Drym, who, from the nasty look on his grey face, was clearly relishing the prospect of bashing Dribble with Spikey as he raised the sharp stick as high as he could above his head.

Dribble looked up at Drym and Spikey, and whimpered once more.

He hoped the beating wouldn't hurt too much.

The little dust-dog closed his tired eyes… and waited for his sad and lonely life to end.

FOUR

Misty's Last Gasp

Misty was gasping for air.

He was starting to lose consciousness.

Everything was going grey inside his head.

Then, as he took one last gasp of breath in a desperate attempt to fill his lungs, he heard the muffled sound of a kindly voice.

'Come on, kitty. Let's get you off there. I need this compost for the castle.'

'MEEOWWWWW! HSSSSSSS!'

Meow was not at all pleased to be moved from her warm and comfortable position on the compost heap. And the greedy cat was definitely not pleased to be parted from her mouse-dessert. The fat feline dug her claws into Mr Bude's big strong hands and bit his finger. He didn't flinch. His skin was as tough as leather from years of gardening, and he was very kind.

'Now, now, puss; that's not very nice, is it? Well I never. Biting and scratching old uncle Bart. Well I never. That won't do. Won't do at all.'

With that, he gently put Meow on the ground and pushed her on her way: 'Off you go then.'

Misty found he could now move his legs. He crawled beneath the surface of the compost, the Golden Key still securely held between his teeth.

Bartholomew Bude, or Bart as he was known to his friends, began humming a tune as he picked up his shovel.

Misty peered out through some strands of straw, just in time to see the sharp blade of the shovel coming straight at him!

Scrunch!

Luckily, he was able to duck, and the blade went just over his head as it sliced into the compost.

With the next shovelling, Misty found *himself* on the shovel, being carried upwards. He was then thrown through the air before landing in the cart with the rest of the compost.

After quite a bit more shovelling, the gardener's task was finished. Misty reflected on his situation: he was thawing out and could move his limbs quite freely. And, he had finally escaped from that horrible…

Pmff!

Suddenly, there was a muffled sound above him and he felt a slight vibration. Something had landed very quietly on top of the compost.

Misty peered through the straw once more.

FIVE

Roasting Gnomes

Old Oaky swayed his branches even more frantically as the raging fire roared up the sides of his thick trunk.

Plumper, who was nearest the flames, was getting hotter and hotter by the second. Billowing smoke engulfed him and he knew that he and his friends would soon choke to death if they didn't do something… and fast!

'Swinger,' he shouted along the line of upsified gnomes, 'can you swing to the top of the branch?'

'I'll try.'

Swinger started swinging backwards and forwards on the slitherrope that held his feet.

'Higher! Higher!' shouted the other gnomes.

After six full swings, Swinger made one really huge effort and, suddenly, he was above the branch.

Thudd!

He landed with a thud, right down on top of the slitherrope.

'Hssssssssss!'

The rope hissed as it released Swinger's feet from its grasp and dropped from the branch to the ground.

Now the brave little gnome went along the line, stomping on every one of the slitherropes in turn.

Stomp! 'Hssssssssss!' Stomp! 'Hssssssssss!' Stomp! 'Hssssssssss!'

Each rope hissed as it let go of the branch, and all the gnomes were soon lying on the ground next to their little red bobble hats.

Without Warleggan to tell them what to do, the slitherropes writhed about in confusion amongst the gnomes. Then, suddenly, as if they had made a simultaneous collective decision, they each released their grip on the ankles of the gnomes and slithered off into the long grass.

'Quickly,' shouted Greenfingers, 'we need to put the fire out or Old Oaky will burn to death.'

Seven of the gnomes ran for the water pump and filled buckets. Prickle ran indoors.

Trust her not to help, thought Plumper. However, a few seconds later, Prickle emerged carrying some big blankets. She ran towards Old Oaky as fast as she could. The seven other gnomes followed her towards their tree-friend with their heavy water buckets.

Plumper helped Prickle smother the flames with the blankets. The other gnomes threw the water from the buckets as high as they could up the trunk and, all of a sudden, the fire was extinguished.

All the gnomes looked at Old Oaky's burnt bark and sobbed.

But Greenfingers had some words of encouragement, which cheered everyone up considerably.

'Don't worry,' he comforted, 'with a little care and attention, and my special Soothing Solution, his bark will grow back and he'll be fine in no time.'

Old Oaky swayed his upper branches as if he were very pleased to hear it.

All the gnomes cheered with happiness.

'HOORRRAYYY!'

SIX

Wake Up, Miss Perfect

'Wake up, Miss Perfect, please wake up,' pleaded the children as they shook the limp and lifeless body of their teacher amidst the burning ruins of Towan Blystra Primary School.

'Oooohh!' Miss Perfect sighed as she came around for a few moments. 'Bombs in the sky. Fire. Take cover, children…

'Oooohh!' The teacher sighed again as she lost consciousness once more.

Joharvy Par knew it was time to act, to take charge. He was in *Year 6,* and the oldest of the group by far. Perhaps, because of the imminent danger to the younger children, Joh began thinking very clearly.

'Right then,' he commanded, 'all of you, into the caretaker's shed on the other side of the playground. Go on then, quick as you can.' With that, the young Kernowkids ran over to the shed.

When they had all squeezed into it, Joharvy closed the door behind them, with a final stern warning: 'I'm going to get help. Stay here until I get back, or an adult you know comes for you.'

Most of the children left inside the hut were only six or seven years old. It was dark and they were very frightened. Maisy March, who was only four, was trembling.

'Errherrrrrr.'

A trickle of wee-wee ran down her leg and she began to sob, setting off some of the other children, who started crying too.

'Errherrrrr. Errherrrrrr. Errherrrrrr.'

Outside, Joh Par could hear the crying and sobbing coming from inside the hut as he tried to decide on a plan of action. Then he remembered that Trerice House was just up the hill from the school. Major Merrymeet will know what to do, the young boy hoped as he hurried off towards the big house.

SEVEN

The Blystra Bay Rip Curlers

Horrrrrrrrnnnnnn! Horrrrrrrrnnnnnn! Horrrrrrrrnnnnnn!

As Hughey the huer continued to sound his horn across Blystra Bay, five of the invading ramdragons swooped in low.

Down at the beach, about two dozen teenagers – the *Blystra Bay Rip Curlers* – were doing what they did most early mornings… they were surfing the crashing waves.

All the Rip Curlers had multi-coloured surfsliders; boards made specially for sliding over the surf. They wore multi-coloured surfsuits to match their surfsliders. The Blystra Bay Rip Curlers rode the biggest waves and were totally fearless. Their surfsliders and surfsuits all had a special ***BBRC*** motif on them, to show they belonged to the gang.

Cule Chegwidden was leader of the Rip Curlers. He was renowned throughout Kernowland as the coolest champion surfer of them all. His gang was also known as 'Cule's Crew', and they had their own way of speaking. They would say things which their parents didn't understand, like: 'that's so pants, geez.'

Many of the teenagers in Kernowland tried to be a bit different from their parents; although they usually became exactly like them when they got older and had children of their own.

Whhhhzzzzzzzzzzzzzzzzzzzzzzzzz!

As he dived, a Shlew warrior released a walnut-sized round stone from his slingshot. The whizzing missile hit Cule's cousin, Chip Chegwidden, on the back of the head, knocking him instantly unconscious. Chip fell off his board into the water, where he floated face down, with his arms and legs outstretched.

One of the ramdragons, Drock, put his front legs forward, extended his razortalons and sunk them deep into Ricky Trevithick's shoulders, lifting him straight off his surfslider and into the air.

'Arrrgghhhhh!' The terrified young man screamed in shock as Drock climbed high above the sea. Ricky's friends watched in horror as the ramdragon then dropped him, and he plummeted down, waving his arms and legs wildly, before hitting the water with a huge splash.

Drone, the fastest of the ramdragons, belched out a huge fire breath as he glided along just above the waves, knocking two of the Rip Curlers off their surfsliders with his massive, out-stretched wings.

Horrrrrrrrrnnnnnn! Horrrrrrrrrnnnnnn! Horrrrrrrrrnnnnnn!

Cule, on first hearing the warning horn, looked behind just in time to see a ramdragon diving straight at him with its razortalons outstretched.

Luckily, just at that moment, the surfing champ had caught a huge tunnel wave. He rode inside the wave and just managed to avoid a barrage of slingstones by zigzagging furiously as he surfed.

At the last possible moment, just as the ramdragon was readying to grab his shoulders with its razor-sharp talons, Cule did a forward somersault and dived deep into the safety of the underwater.

EIGHT

Brave Masai

On seeing Tizzie's plight, Jack and Masai exchanged a look, and knew instinctively what to do.

Masai ran towards the side of the ship where Tizzie had been blown overboard.

Jack picked up a rope and muttered a spell under his breath. The rope instantly formed itself into a lasso. As Masai ran, Jack swung the looped rope above his head and released it in the direction of his tall friend.

It was a great shot. The loop fell right down over Masai's shoulders. Still running, the tall boy managed to pull on the rope to make it tight around his waist, just as he dived over the ship's rail and into the roaring sea.

The piranhasharks were almost upon them.

With two strokes and strong kicks of his feet, Masai had reached Tizzie. He grabbed hold around her waist with both of his long, muscular arms.

Seeing that Masai had a secure hold on Tizzie, Jack and Hans gripped the rope tightly and ran backwards across the deck as fast as they could.

Tizzie and Masai were pulled through the water towards the ship at great speed.

'Pull faster! PLEEAASSE!'

The screaming girl could now see the jagged teeth in the gaping mouths of the hungry fish as they sped towards her.

Just as the piranahsharks reached them… the rope pulled Masai and Tizzie out of the water.

'NOOHHHHHHH!'

Tizzie screamed even louder as she saw one of the fish fly into the air and bite Masai's left foot, before dropping back with a splash into the foaming surf.

She felt Masai's whole body stiffen with the pain… but he made no sound.

NINE

Invasion From The North

Horrrrrrrrrrnnnnnn! Horrrrrrrrrrnnnnnn! Horrrrrrrrrrnnnnnn!

Dashing choughateer, Perry Perranporth, heard Huey's warning horn blowing as he read his morning newspaper, the *Daily Packet*.

INVASION!!!

I must raise the alarm.

Remembering his training, Perry ran into his garden and quickly fired off two flameflares high into the air to let others know that an invasion had begun.

Then he loaded his weapons and took off on Chock, who had been resting in his hangarhouse in the field behind the cottage.

Flares and alarm beacons were soon going off all over Kernowland, warning the Kernowfolk that they were under attack.

Each and every Kernowlander volunteered for national military service as soon as they were old enough. They were all members of the Kernowland Defence Force: *The Guardians of Kernow*.

'ONEN HAG OLL!'

'ONEN HAG OLL!'

'ONEN HAG OLL!'

Everywhere, as soon as they heard the rousing rallying cry, the men and women of Kernowland armed themselves and left their homes and work places to repel The Invader.

The Land, Sea, and Air Guardians quickly joined their regiments, fleets, and squadrons.

Admiral Crumplehorn ordered his ships to sail.
The donkeyteers rode out.
The infantry marched.
The dolphineers swam.
And the choughateers flew.

TEN

The Single Shot

'Wooooowoowooowooowooooooooo!'

The desert riders were approaching rapidly.

Louis made up his mind… he'd have to risk going back to the Golden Cavern.

It was his only chance of escape.

Louis' hand shook as he fumbled in his pocket and pulled out the Golden Key.

He knew that all he had to do was touch its end on the sand and say, *Golden Cavern, by the power of Godolphin*, and he would be instantly transported back through the Crystal Door to the cavern beneath Kernow Castle.

But the young boy was in such a tremulous panic that he dropped the key on the sand.

Just at that moment, the desert wind blew harder and a thick cloud of sandy dust engulfed him.

He watched in horror as the key sank beneath the shifting grains.

'Wooooowoowooowooowooooooooo!'

The shrieking men were almost upon him.

'Bang!'

A single shot rang out.

ELEVEN

Choughateers

Along with Perry, thirty-two other choughateers had very rapidly got airborne as soon as they had seen or heard the invasion warnings.

The thirty-three brave pilots had now grouped on their skymounts in the skies above Towan Blystra.

Perry's heart began to pound inside his chest as the defenders made ready to engage the enemy.

Although hopelessly outnumbered by the Shlew ramraiders on their red ramdragons, the young choughateers bravely followed their Squadron Leader, Freddie 'Iceman' Fowey, towards the flying invaders now dropping a hail of blazeballs on the town.

Gripping his legs tightly around his chough in readiness for battle, Perry's heart pounded even harder as he spotted the nine biggest ramdragons at the rear of the enemy attack force.

He knew the nine cage-carriers would be aiming to land their carnivorous cargo on Blystra Cliffs.

The trogs just couldn't be allowed to reach the town… every living thing would be eaten.

Iceman Fowey had also seen the danger.

'Get the trogs!' he shouted, as he flew close to Perry. 'Take two chaps with you.'

TWELVE

Nevernevernever Give Up

CABOOM! Suddenly, Dribble heard a very loud noise.

But he didn't feel anything; not a stab, not a bash, not a thing. The little dust-dog opened his eyes.

To his amazement, there, on the ground beside him, lay Drym and Wendron, both apparently unconscious.

'*Nevernevernever give up*, is what my father used to say,' said Clevercloggs from a few paces away, with a wide grin and a twinkle in his eye. He was holding a short, thick, stick-like object in his hand. Dribble noticed that a similar stick was lying near Drym and Wendron.

'Cleversticks,' informed the old gnome, as he lay on the road, still trapped by one leg under Heavyfeather's prostrate form. 'Bangers, Clouders, Fizzers, I've made all sorts of these weapons.'

Dribble thought Clevercloggs was very clever to make cleversticks that could knock out both Drym and Wendron at the same time. And he was very relieved to have been saved from a fatal beating with Spikey.

The panting dachshund pulled himself over to Clevercloggs, dragging his two hind legs, still entangled with the snarebolas, along behind him.

Scrrrrrrrrrrrrrrrrrrrrrrrr.

Clevercloggs had just removed the snarebolas from around Dribble's back legs when they heard the buzzing of the Skyscooter once more.

Warleggan!

The warty warlock had made a wide turn and was now racing towards them from behind Clevercloggs, with smoke billowing from the exhaust of his flying machine.

Taking aim as he flew along at incredible speed a few feet off the ground, Warleggan threw a stunstone with deadly accuracy. It hit Clevercloggs squarely on the back of the head… and the old gnome flopped to the ground.

Little Dribble had now just about had enough. He was very cross indeed.

'GRRRRRRRRRR!'

Growling fiercely, the little dust-dog bravely leapt straight at their attacker, grabbing the warlock's Warcoat with his teeth… and then letting it go very quickly.

This was just enough contact to cause Warleggan to spin around and around and around in the air, before bouncing along the road and crashing into a tree, at the foot of which he now lay crumpled and unconscious.

Dribble padded over to Clevercloggs and Heavyfeather, and licked their faces with his slobbery tongue until they were covered in drool. For some reason, this seemed to have the desired effect because, although still a little groggy, swan and gnome were both soon awake again.

'We need to be away from here without delay,' advised Clevercloggs, as he wiped his face dry with his sleeve. 'These three troublemakers will soon wake up… and I think we can safely say they're all going to be in a *very* bad mood indeed.'

THIRTEEN

Trog Trouble

High in the sky, Bite, one of the trogs in the carry cages, was not at all happy.

Trog fleas, with which he was permanently infested, were much bigger than ordinary fleas, and they really did nip quite badly. In consequence, Bite's hairy hand was roaming all over his body; he was itching and scratching himself everywhere.

Trogs had very long and straight head hair. It fell from the top of their heads, around the back and sides as well as down the front, so that it covered their faces, making it quite difficult for them to see. They also had wiry, matted fur all over the rest of their bodies.

As he scratched, Bite peered through his hair at the next cage and saw his brother, Chew, staring at him. Chew was itching and scratching too.

Bite and Chew were twins, but did not like each other at all. They were always fighting. At every opportunity, the trog twins would pinch and scratch and hit each other with their clubs.

Just then, Bite spied three Choughateers coming out of the sun in attack formation: 'Trroggaarhh!'

Then Chew saw them: 'Trroggaarhh!'

The hairy trogs roared loudly and rattled the bars of their carry cages furiously.

Perry and his two comrades, Chester Camborne and Wilbur Wadebridge, had flown high into the sky. They were now diving

27

down to attack the nine trailing ramdragons carrying the trogs.

Every chough went into battle with a big crossbow attached between its shoulders. Each crossbow fired two bolts at a time. As Chock dived at lightning speed towards the target, Perry wound back the firing mechanism, aimed carefully… and released the bolts.

Thudd! Thudd!

The pointed missiles shot through the air, each piercing, with a dull thud, the long red neck of the leading cage-carrying ramdragon.

'Roarrrhhhh!'

The ramdragon roared in pain and shock, and the great red beast puffed out a huge, trailing breath of smoke as it plummeted down towards the sea.

Chester and Wilbur fired their own crossbow bolts at the next two cage-carriers. Moments after they were hit, both of the ramdragons began spiral dives towards the sea, with smoke billowing from their mouths.

The other Shlew ramraiders returned fire with their slingshots, bows, and other weapons, but their lumbering steeds were no match for the lightning-fast and highly manoeuvrable choughs.

With their advantage of surprise, the three choughateers had soon dispatched the nine cage-carrying ramdragons down towards the water. Six of the ramdragons crashed into the waves; and six trogs sank under the surface, quite a way out to sea.

But three of the cages smashed into the beach, breaking up on impact. Trogs are very tough and all three survived, a little dazed but otherwise unhurt.

Although none of them was very clever, the three half-starved trogs soon realised they would now have to climb the cliffs in order to get at the promised food.

'Trroggaarhhhhhhhhhhhhhhhhhhhh!'
'Trroggaarhhhhhhhhhhhhhhhhhhhh!'
'Trroggaarhhhhhhhhhhhhhhhhhhhh!'

Bite, Chew, and Gnaw each stood up on the beach to their full nine feet, swinging their clubs in the air and beating them on the sand as they roared their disapproval. Now they were very angry as well as very hungry.

A group of three or more trogs is called a 'trouble'. The trouble of trogs began to march slowly up the beach, all frantically rubbing and scratching their flea bites as they went.

On reaching Blystra Cliffs, they stuck their clubs in their belts and began climbing with clawed hands and feet that seemed ideally suited for the purpose.

As the trogs scaled the cliffs, saliva dripped from their mouths and they smacked their lips and rolled their long brown tongues around their tearing teeth in anticipation of the feeding feast to come.

FOURTEEN

Crafty Cat

Misty's worst fears were confirmed. Meow had climbed a tree and jumped from an overhanging branch into the cart, landing softly on the compost, so as not to alert Mr Bude.

The trembling mouse could see the crafty cat was searching slowly and silently through the compost with her nose and paws. Misty burrowed a little further down.

But the rustling alerted Meow.

Mmmmm, the mouse is moving now, thought the cat.

Ready to eat!

The ferocious feline bounded around the compost, sending her front right paw deep down through the layers in different places as she tried to get her long sharp claws into Misty.

Quivering with fear, the little mouse burrowed still further. But he had now reached the floor of the cart. There was nowhere else to run or hide.

Meow spied her meal, parted the compost… and made ready to pounce.

'Shooo! Shooo!'

Luckily, at that very moment, Mr Bude decided to look behind to see the splendid view of Eden Valley.

Immediately spotting Meow, he shooed her away.

Meow had no choice. She knew Mr Bude would only throw her off if she didn't go of her own accord. So she reluctantly leapt off the cart, leaving her dessert delicacy behind.

'Phew!' Misty sighed with relief and settled down to have a well-earned rest. There had certainly been enough excitement in the hours since he was in the cellar at the Polperro Inn to last him a lifetime.

All he could think about now was the fate of his little friend Louis.

He had heard Mr Bude mention 'the castle'.

So far as he knew, that was where Louis would be heading if he had survived the brainboiler incident.

As he drifted off to sleep, Misty hoped and hoped that Louis had survived and that the cart would take him to Kernow Castle.

FIFTEEN

The Other Road

As they left the road and began walking through heavy mud, Clevercloggs outlined his thoughts to his companions.

'By the look of that dark mushroom cloud above Kernow Castle, we're already too late to warn the King about traitors and invasions.

'But I have to get to the castle to find out more about what's happened. Only then will I be able to make a proper plan.

'First, we'll make our way across these fields to the other road into Truro.

'Then, Dribble, you must lead Heavyfeather back along that road to Washaway Wood. Drym and his cronies are unlikely to suspect that you've gone back there. I'll just have to get around on my sticks.

'If I wait under cover at the roadside, there's sure to be someone friendly on the road who can give me a lift to Kernow Castle. I know someone there who, whatever has happened, will definitely still be loyal to Kernowland.'

Although they didn't want to leave their friend, Dribble and Heavyfeather nodded to show that they understood and agreed. The old gnome was very wise and he always seemed to know what was best.

Fzzzzzzzz. Flashhh!

It was at that moment that they saw flameflares lighting up the sky.

'Invasion warnings,' mused Clevercloggs. 'So it has begun. Come on my friends, we must make haste. I need to get to the castle as soon as possible.'

With that, Clevercloggs, Heavyfeather, and Dribble continued on their arduous trudge through mud and hedges in the direction of the other road.

SIXTEEN

Evile's Armada

Kernowland's courage and staunch determination to defend itself was legendary throughout Erthwurld. Even with the Forcesphere destroyed, the tiny kingdom would still be considered a formidable foe by any aggressor.

Evile's generals and the ten traitors had, therefore, secretly planned a 'blitzkrieg' – an invasion of such ferocity and over-whelming odds that it would be over in one day.

Today was that day: *DARKNESS DAY*.

Just minutes after the northern air assault by the Shlew on their ramdragons, the massed ships of Evile's Armada sailed over the horizons to the west and south of Kernowland, thus entering her sovereign waters… a blatant act of WAR!

In the west, off the coast of Land's End, were the Vikings in their longships. They carried with them the fearsome Highland Tocs and the ferocious Eriemen. From the south, all along the coast from the River Tamar to Penzance, sailed the warships of the Moors, the Gauls, and the Guerreros.

At the same time, on the eastern border, the largest land army ever raised advanced on Kernowland. The huge cannon of the Angles were hauled up and ranged opposite the northern stretch of the Great Wall. And, all along the hills facing the southern stretch of the wall, were the Zulus and their Animal Army of Acirfa.

The stage was set for the greatest battle Erthwurld had seen in a very long time.

SEVENTEEN

Little Toe, Little Girl

'Get them slaves aboard,' shouted Captain Pigleg as he saw Tizzie and Masai being hauled up the side of the ship. Three strong pirates helped Jack and Hans pull on the rope until the two rescuees were back on the deck.

Purgy looked at Masai's foot.

'This slave is damaged, Cap'n. Shall we chuck 'im overboard?'

'Don't think that'll be necessary,' answered the captain. 'He's still good for bait, don't you agree, mates?'

'Aye, aye, Cap'n,' roared all the pirates in unison.

With that, Jack and Hans helped Masai to hop across the deck towards the hold.

They used the lasso to lower him down below, where he lay quietly on the wooden boards, whilst Jack tended to his wound.

Tizzie looked at the blood-soaked bandage that Jack had applied. She couldn't believe that Masai was still not complaining about the pain. He was actually smiling.

'I'm afraid you've lost your little toe,' commiserated Jack.

'Yes, I see that is so,' said Masai, as he gave Tizzie a big grin that showed all his shiny white teeth.

'But we didn't lose the little girl!'

EIGHTEEN

What About Gran?

Cule could hold his breath no longer. As he surfaced from the relative safety of the underwater, he soon saw the cruel carnage that had been unleashed by the ramdragons.

All of his friends had been attacked.

'Help!'

'Help!'

'Help!'

Cries for help could be heard from every direction.

There were smashed surfsliders and floating bodies everywhere. The sea was stained with ruby red patches of blood.

Luckily, a few of the Rip Curlers had escaped with only minor cuts and bruises. Cule, and any others who were able, swam around collecting and helping the seriously injured, who all moaned and groaned as they were brought ashore.

As far as he could make out, at least three of his friends, including sweet Zoe Zennor, were very obviously dead. Others were badly injured, a few with serious firebreath burns.

Whilst tending to the wounded as best he could, something made Cule look up towards the cliffs.

In the distance, he could just make out the trouble of trogs starting to scale the rock face. He knew instantly where the hairy beasts were going and what they would do to the townsfolk.

They'll be eating *everyone*, he thought.

What about gran? She's at home making pastys!

NINETEEN

Unjust Rewards

Wendron, Warleggan, and Drym all awoke at the same time. They were still a bit groggy. The wrinkled witch spoke first.

'Look, above the castle. That mushroom cloud is evidence enough. The Young Master has succeeded!'

'Let's get over there as soon as we can... for our rewards,' said Drym.

'Yes,' agreed Wendron, 'and well-deserved they'll be too. I'll send Craw ahead with a note announcing our arrival. And I'll warn the Young Master that Clevercloggs has been interfering.'

'But you said you wouldn't say anything about the writing in my diary, oh yes you did,' squirmed Drym, concerned that he may not get what he'd been promised if his scribblings were reported to his leader.

'Don't worry, dirt-boy, your secret's safe with me... for now at least.'

The trio of traitors set off on their way to the castle in the Skycycle.

It wasn't far, so, rather than fly, Wendron decided to taxi the contraption along the road.

As the tricycle veered and bounced along the way – due to the earlier warping of the front wheel – Drym thought happy thoughts about finally being granted his slaving franchise... and about how much money he was going to make by selling all the children into slavery.

When they were about halfway to the castle, Craw returned, bringing his mistress a reply note and castle pass in his beak.

'Gooood! I was right. The Young Master's plan has worked and we are all expected as honoured guests.'

On arrival at the gate, they showed the pass to the guard.

'We have an audience with King Manaccan,' announced Warleggan, rather self-importantly.

The guard had already been told to expect them, and they were immediately escorted to the Dome Tower.

TWENTY

Dolphineers To The Rescue

Just as he was trying to decide what to do, Cule saw a very welcome sight.

Dolphineers!

Bella Bodella was the leader of the local squadron of dolphineers. Only just eighteen, she was also 'Miss Towan Blystra', having won the town's annual beauty queen contest two months earlier.

The dolphineers had been on training exercise just outside Blystra Bay, when they had heard Hughey's warning horn.

Every dolphineer was taught to respond quickly to the plight of anyone in trouble, without fear or hesitation. So, when she heard the warning horn, Bella knew exactly what to do. She had immediately led her dartingdolphin, Dash, towards the sound; with her squadron following on close behind.

The dolphineers, all brave young women, sat back in their saddles and held on to the reins tightly as their dartingdolphins raced towards the danger. Each of them readied their stingers in case there was going to be a fight.

Stingers were thin poles, like lances, with a special crystal on the end that had been charged with eelectricity, an awesome source of natural power, which had originally been discovered – from a long and close study of electric eels – by Clevercloggs the Explorer, many years before.

Each dolphineer carried a supply of crystal ammunition in a

special waterproof pouch, which was hung around the neck. Some of the crystals were green, others were red. The green crystals carried just enough eelectric charge for knocking someone over, or occasionally out, and were often used to arrest people who needed to go to prison or to stop them being bad or disorderly, such as drunken sailors.

The red crystals, however, carried a lethal charge and killed an opponent instantly. They were for fiercer fighting, like a battle.

As she approached on Dash, Bella was very pleased to see that Cule Chegwidden was unhurt. Like many other girls in Kernowland, she was very much in love with the handsome surfing champion.

However, when she saw the seriousness of what had happened to the other Rip Curlers, Bella's pleasure turned to anger.

'Terrible, just terrible,' she mumbled under her breath.

But – after the initial shock – she quickly composed herself and immediately ordered her squadron to help all those who had been hurt.

As Bella rode on Dash towards the beach, she saw Cule running from the sand into the waves, shouting and gesturing frantically.

'Look there. Climbing the cliffs…

'TROGS!'

TWENTY-ONE

Spiderscorpion

Whzzzzzzzzzzzzzzzzzzzzzzzzzzzzzzzzzzzzzzz!

A bullet whizzed over Louis' head.

SCREEEEEEECHHH!

He heard a deafening screech behind him.

Turning quickly about, the young boy looked up to see a fifteen-foot long scorpion's stinger, coiled in readiness to attack him.

The stinger was attached to a massive black creature, with eight hairy legs and four huge eyes; a spiderscorpion.

The first shot had hit the stinger and momentarily stunned the creature.

Bang!

Whzzzzzzzzzzzzzzzzzzzzzzzzzzzzzzzzzzzzzzz!

SCREEEEEEECHHH!

Now another shot rang out. It hit the stinger again and the spiderscorpion screeched once more.

Fmppp! Squelch!

As Louis reached for his catapult, a spinning scimitar thudded into the creature, right between two of its staring eyes.

'Wooooowoowooowooowooooooooo!'

Within moments, the shrieking men had surrounded the spiderscorpion on their camels, and were attacking it from all sides with their curved swords, lances, and muskets.

Stnnnng!

The spiderscorpion struck. Its stinger pierced the neck of one of the camels. The camel fell instantly to the sand… dead.

The man on the camel's back jumped clear as his mount was downed. With incredible athleticism and bravery, he leapt on the spiderscorpion's back, swung his sword and chopped off the stinger with one swipe.

Dark brown, putrid-smelling blood squirted everywhere.

Seconds later, the spiderscorpion was dead.

All the men turned to look at Louis.

The leader dropped his sandveil to reveal his sun-weathered, Brownskin face.

TWENTY–TWO

Esrom Code

When Bella saw the trogs climbing the cliffs, she knew she had to do something… and fast.

Looking skywards, she saw that the choughateers were fighting the Shlew ramraiders in a fierce air battle. Thinking quickly, Bella reached for her make-up mirror. She reflected the rays of the sun in a series of dots and dashes using *Esrom Code*, a communication system named after its inventor, Luemas Esrom.

Choughateer, Peter Par – who was flying on his female chough, Chick – saw the twinkling dots and dashes from below. He read the message aloud:

'T-h-e t-r-o-g-s a-r-e c-l-i-m-b-i-n-g t-h-e c-l-i-f-f-s.'

Quickly locating the trogs, the pilot acted decisively.

'Okay girl, down there, at two o'clock. Let's get stuck in.'

With that, Peter leaned forward and slightly to the right to put Chick into a controlled, but very steep, spiral dive. They had to lose a lot of height very quickly because the trogs were already halfway up the cliff face.

Like all choughateers, Peter carried various weapons on board, some of them held in two saddlebags. He had three blinding blankets. These were large squares of cloth with four stones tied by bits of thin rope to the corners and one stone tied to the centre.

Now flying parallel to the cliff face at the level of the uppermost trog, Peter held the centre stone and whirled his arm above his head. The weight of the other stones opened up the blanket above him. Peter guided Chick as close to the cliff as he could and, with a huge effort, released the blinding blanket in the direction of Gnaw, who had climbed highest. The blanket wrapped around the trog's head.

'Trroggaarrrhhhh', roared Gnaw in anger, grabbing at the blanket with both hands to try to remove it.

Gnaw soon realised his mistake. With *both* hands on the blanket, he had *no* hands on the cliff! With a curious expression on his face, he began to fall backwards, and went through three somersaults in the air before crashing on to the beach with a crunch.

'Splendid work, Chick,' congratulated Peter, happy with their first attack. 'But we have to go in again. There are two more of those hairy beasts on the cliffs, and they'll eat everyone in the town if we don't stop them. We'll try another blanket.'

Peter and Chick flew out over the bay in a tight circuit, so that they could again position themselves parallel to the cliff for a second attack. But this time, as Peter released the blanket, Bite simply ducked and held on tightly to the cliff face, and the blanket missed its target. After another circuit, Peter came in for a third pass with his last blinding blanket, again trying to wrap it around Bite's head. Bite ducked once more.

'That top trog's cleverer, Chick,' shouted Peter in exasperation, 'I'll try my lance on the next one down.'

After the tightest circuit he could possibly get Chick to fly, Peter withdrew his lance from its holster, slotted it tightly in position under his right arm, put his head down, gritted his teeth and flew as fast as he could at Chew.

'Tally ho, this is for Kernowland!' he shouted, as Chick flew parallel to the cliff once again, this time with her right wing pointing towards the ground and her left wing to the clouds. Holding on to the reins as tightly as he could with his left hand, Peter steadied his lance and aimed it straight at Chew's ribs.

SQUELCH! SNAP!

'Trroggaarhh!' screamed the trog, as the lance squelched into his flesh, snapping in half as it lodged in his midriff.

'Direct hit, well done Chi… uughh…'

Before Peter could finish his congratulations to Chick, Chew had jumped off the cliff and landed right on top of them.

'Trroggaarhh!'

The roaring trog sank his teeth deep into Chick's neck. Try as she might, there was no way that the chough could fly with a trog hanging on to her throat by its tearing teeth. Peter, Chick, and Chew were knotted together as they plummeted, heads-over-wings, towards the ground.

Crack! Crack! Crack! Crunch!

There was a series of cracks and a big crunch as the tangled mass of hair, feathers, legs, arms, and wings hit the rocks. Blood poured from Peter's head. He couldn't move his legs. Facing the sky, he could see the remaining trog climbing ever closer towards the top of the cliff. A tear filled his eye as he looked at Chick's throat, which was torn open. Her eyes were closed and she was very obviously dead.

'At least we got two of them,' he whispered, as he patted Chick's broken wing. 'Well done, brave girl.'

Peter was proud that he and Chick had done their duty for Kernowland as best they could. But their bravery had cost them both dear. Peter wept another tear for Chick, coughing and choking as he gasped for breath.

Then the brave choughateer slowly shut his own eyes… for the very last time.

TWENTY-THREE

Sheik Akbar Sharif

'Greetings little warrior,' said the tallest of the desert riders, with a kindly smile. 'I am Akbar Sharif, a Sheik of Sandland.'

Louis immediately liked Akbar. The sheik and his men had obviously saved him from the spiderscorpion and they seemed to want to help him further.

'I am Louis,' he replied, 'a Prince of Forestland.'

'And how do you come to be here in our Desert of Arahas, many kiloms from anywhere?'

Louis told the sheik everything. All about how he had gone to the White Light Ceremony with Mr Sand and how Manaccan had killed the King, and Violothan had destroyed the Forcesphere and blown up the Prism Chamber. He also told how he had planned to rescue his sister by going to Jungleland through the Crystal Door, but that he must have said the words wrongly and ended up here in Sandland. Louis finished his story with the words: 'Then I saw you and your men and I was so scared at first that I dropped the key in the sand.'

Akbar Sharif had listened intently all the way through.

'Well, Prince Louis, I can now tell you that my fellows and I are the Desert Riders of Arahas. We are also members of RAE, the Rebels Against Evile. You may be surprised to learn that we have worked with King Kernow and Mr Sand on many occasions for the greater good of Erthwurld. It is sad indeed to hear that Kernowland has lost its main defence against an invasion by the

Empire. The courageous little kingdom has always been such a shining beacon of light and hope for us all. But perhaps our paths have crossed for a reason, little warrior. And perhaps – by the Will and Grace of Omni – we may still wrest victory from the depths of despair.'

Louis smiled as Akbar put a protective arm around his shoulder.

'Come, let us find the Golden Key quickly. We must make it back to Camp Oasis before nightfall. The Great Simoom will be blowing much more fiercely soon and it is not wise to be outside your tent in such a sandstorm, especially after dark when the desert carnivores go hunting.'

'Um… what sort of *carnivores*?' asked Louis, who was – perhaps understandably after his experience with Monstro – more than a little worried by *that* word.

'Well, there are lots of them,' answered Akbar. 'You've already met the giant spiderscorpion. Then there are the other mutant gigantics, such as the sabretoothed sandcats and silverstriped hyenas. And, of course, most dangerous of all are the fourfang sidewinders… snakes that can outpace a running man and swallow a camel and rider whole.'

Louis immediately started looking for the Golden Key; he didn't relish the thought of meeting any more man-eating carnivores one little bit.

After a few minutes, one of Akbar's men found the key in the sand. Louis put the precious object back in his pocket as Akbar spoke again: 'Once we are safe in our tents, we will see what we can do to help you rescue Princess Tizzie.'

Louis beamed and nodded to show he thought this was a splendid idea.

As they set off, riding on camels towards the sun, the brave young boy felt so lucky that he had met Akbar Sharif, the kind sheik.

Although he now understood that he'd made a big mistake when using the Crystal Door – and so ended up here in Sandland – he considered it a great stroke of good fortune that he would soon have another chance to rescue Tizzie.

TWENTY-FOUR

Discusfrisbees

Cule watched in horror as Peter and Chick plummeted to their deaths at the hands of the trogs. All he could think of now was saving his gran from becoming trog food.

Amongst his many other famous achievements, Cule was the junior boxing, fencing, and wrestling champion of Kernowland, so he was a very good fighter. But this situation was different. He had never had to fight for *real* before. It was all so new and sudden, and a bit of a shock to him.

However, the versatile young champion knew one thing for certain: he now had to think and act decisively. This was war!

Cule ran to a big canvas bag lying on the beach. He picked it up and hurried to the base of the cliff. Here he took a large, flat, heavy wooden disk out of it: a discusfrisbee, or 'disbee' for short.

Cule was also junior disbee-throwing champion of Kernowland, and he and his friends often practised using the weapons on the beach, as part of their training to be Land Guardians. His idea was to knock the trog off the cliff with a disbee. Taking aim at Bite, he brought his arm back and threw the metal-rimmed weapon as hard as he could. Disbees were quite heavy and he had to summon his best throw to launch it far enough.

Clunk! He scored a direct hit, and the whirling weapon made contact – with a dull clunk – on the back of Bite's head. The trog was so surprised that it nearly let go of its grip on the cliff. But it held on.

The young champ knew he didn't have much time as the trog was still climbing. There were five more disbees in the bag. He reached in and pulled another out. Taking careful aim, he threw again with all his might.

This time, Bite was ready. He saw the missile coming and held on to the rocks with one clawpaw, whilst catching the spinning disk in mid-air with his other.

'Trroggaarhh!' he roared triumphantly, as he bit clean through the wood and metal and spat the chunk out, before tossing the disk away and watching it drop towards the beach.

Seizing his chance, while the trog was distracted, Cule reached into the bag again and threw another disbee. This time, the weapon hit the trog squarely between the eyes.

'Trroggaarhh!'

Bite roared again; this time he had really felt the blow... but he *still* held on.

Cule realised that his plan hadn't worked. He'd have to climb.

Down at the water's edge, Bella was still tending the wounded but glancing up every so often to see how Cule was doing.

She saw him signalling that he was going to scale the cliff.

After acknowledging his signal, she watched in horror as Gnaw first stirred, and then began to raise himself up on all fours. Cule was looking towards her and hadn't noticed that the trog was still very much alive.

'Look out, Cule,' shouted Bella, gesturing frantically.

'BEHIND YOU!'

Up the beach, Cule couldn't understand what Bella was saying. He took a few steps towards the sea and cupped one ear with his hand to try to hear better.

'BEHIND YOU!'

Now he could hear! The young champ quickly turned his head around to look in the direction that Bella was pointing. The trog was advancing towards him, waving its hairy arms, curling its long sharp claws, and baring its tearing teeth.

'Whoooooaaahhhh!' Cule exclaimed in fright, then turned and ran back down the beach towards the sea as fast as he could go.

As Cule ran towards her, Bella waved her stinging stick in the air, to show him what she was planning to do. Then she quickly loaded a red killcrystal on to the end of the stinger.

Luckily, Cule was also the junior running champion of Kernowland for all short, middle, and long distances, so he was able to sprint towards the sea at a very good pace.

However, despite the young man's fitness and speed, a nine-foot trog can bound in massive strides, and this one was gaining on him rapidly as he reached the water's edge.

Cule ran into the sea, straight towards Bella.

By now the dolphineer was sitting on Dash, waiting. At the last possible moment, she gave the command: 'Attackattack.'

This was the signal for her dartingdolphin to swim as fast as it could towards the enemy. As Dash accelerated, Bella lowered her stinger so that it became a lance.

Just as the trog reached out to grab him, Cule dived into the water. At that very moment, Bella arrived at full speed on Dash.

Squink! Snap! The stinger snapped from the force of the impact with the trog, throwing Bella from her saddle.

But the killcrystal had done its work. The trog shook all over as the eelectric charge raced through its body. After a few shaking seconds, it fell forwards into the sea, dead.

Cule and Bella cheered and embraced. He kissed her cheek. To his surprise, she took his strong jaw between her hands and kissed him firmly on the lips. It was a very long kiss, but Cule didn't resist. He'd liked Bella for years, ever since they were in the same year at primary school together, but he was uncertain if she liked him back. Now he had his answer, and it gave him the courage to ask her a question.

'When this is all over,' he blurted, 'will you go out with me?'

'Oh yes! Yes, of course I will,' she replied, 'I've always loved you, Cule.'

They kissed again.

Cule suddenly came to his senses and remembered that one of the monsters was still climbing the cliff. Looking in that direction, he saw that the hungry beast was just going over the top. In a couple of minutes, it would be in the town.

'I must save Gran,' he shouted, as he sprinted back up the beach.

'Good luck... and keep safe,' whispered Bella sweetly, as she watched her hero go.

The young dolphineer desperately wanted to help her new boyfriend fight the trogs and save his gran. But she knew her duty was to lead her squadron into battle against The Invader... and she now prepared herself to do just that.

TWENTY-FIVE

The Compost Cart

After waving goodbye to Dribble and Heavyfeather, Clevercloggs waited patiently in the trees beside the other road into Truro. He was hiding in case Wendron, Warleggan, and Drym were still looking for him.

To the gnome's great delight, the first person who came along the road in his compost cart was his good friend, Bart Bude.

Mr Bude had been a good and loyal soldier. A long time ago, he had been a sergeant in the regular Kernish army, and, although well past his best fighting days, Clevercloggs knew the old veteran would still do everything he could for Kernowland.

It was often said that Clevercloggs was so old and well-travelled that he knew everyone in Erthwurld. Whilst this couldn't possibly have been literally true, the old gnome knew so many people that it appeared to all that he did indeed know every single person, animal, and creature in the wurld! He hobbled out of the trees on his sticks as Mr Bude approached.

'Why, if it isn't Clevercloggs, what a lovely surprise on this wonderful day.'

'I'm afraid it's not such a wonderful day, old friend,' said the gnome. He then proceeded to tell Mr Bude everything that had happened, finishing with a recommendation that they make haste: 'So, we'd better get on our way to the castle.'

'Right you are,' agreed Mr Bude, jumping off the cart to lift Clevercloggs onto the back of it.

As Mr Bude climbed back into the driver's seat and started the cart moving, Clevercloggs spoke again: 'When we reach the top of this hill, I have to tell you that you'll see something above Kernow Castle which will sadden your heart.'

At that moment, Misty awoke to the sound of a familiar voice. 'It's Clevercloggs!'

'I'd know that squeak anywhere,' said Clevercloggs in surprise, when he heard his name in Misty's thoughts. The old gnome had long ago learned how to talk to animals. 'Is there a little blue mouse in this cart?'

Misty poked his head out from beneath the straw and scampered over to Clevercloggs with the Golden Key between his teeth, dropping it down in front of his old friend.

Clevercloggs took the key between his fingers and read the Half-Lock Spell along the side. 'This is the key to the Golden Cavern! How did *you* come by it, Misty?'

Clevercloggs relayed everything aloud to Mr Bude as Misty told the wise old gnome all about the unfortunate series of events that had caused him to be in the compost cart.

TWENTY-SIX

CHILDFLESH!

Bite had finally made it over the top of the cliff.

He was hungry… very hungry.

'Trroggaarhh!'

Glancing back out to sea, he roared and beat his chest when he saw that four of the six trogs who had splashed into the water had managed to escape from their cages and swim ashore. Dripping wet, they were now stomping up the beach towards the cliffs.

'Trroggaarhh!'

Down on the beach, all four trogs heard Bite's roar and they all beat their chests and roared back at the same time.

Bite was one of the cleverer trogs. He knew that, if he were quick, he would get the best flesh first. Looking around, he saw he had two choices… the road to town or the road up the hill to Towan Blystra Primary School.

Trogs have a very acute sense of smell.

Snfff. Snfff. Bite sniffed the air and got the faintest whiff of his favourite food: CHILDFLESH!

Hardly able to contain his enthusiasm, the hungry trog bounded up the hill towards the school, with saliva dripping from his mouth in anticipation of the feast to come.

By the time he reached the playground, he was absolutely ravenous for tender, juicy childmeat. Whilst an easy feast would have been Miss Perfect, who was still lying unconscious on the ground, the beast ignored the older meat, and sniffed the air again.

Snfff. Snfff. The smell of young children was much stronger now. The hungry trog knew they were very near.

Just a few feet away, the Kernowkids were all huddled together in the caretaker's little shed, trying to be very quiet.

'Trroggaaaaarrrhhhhh!'

The children all quivered and shook inside the shed as they heard the trog roar. But they knew they mustn't make a sound.

Stmpp. Stmpp. Stmpp. Stmpp.

Now they could hear the monster pacing towards them.

Outside, Bite tried to peer in through the window. Tommy Tremar had cleverly thought to cover the panes with an old newspaper. But the trog was not to be fooled. It trusted its nose. It *knew* the Kernowkids were in the shed.

'Trroggaaaaarrrhhhhh!' Roaring wildly, the huge hungry creature grabbed two corners of the shed and shook the whole thing from side to side, trying to make it fall over.

'HELLLLP!' Inside, the children all screamed for help and started crying.

'Trroggaaaaarrrhhhhh!' The trog roared again as it dug its claws through the wooden door.

Splickkkk!

'HELLLLLLLLLLLP!' The children screamed again as they heard the wood splinter and saw the claws come through to their side of the door.

'TRROGGAAAAARRRHHHH!' The trog pulled with all its might and roared once more.

Squickkkk! There was a horrible squeaking sound as the hinges were wrenched away.

'HELLLLLLLLLLLLLLLLLP!'

'HELLLLLLLLLLLLLLLLLP!'
'HELLLLLLLLLLLLLLLLLP!'

All the children screamed again and again, cowering together at the back of the shed as the trog withdrew its claws from the wooden door and stooped to step inside.

'TRROGGAAAAARRRHHHH!' The monster reached out with a huge hairy clawpaw and lifted little Lorna Luckett off the ground by her pony tail.

'Eeeeeeeeeeeeeeeeeeeeeeee!' The infant shrieked feebly and wiggled her feet backwards and forwards as the monster brought her up close to its flat wide nose and sniffed her skin.

Little Lorna looked deep into the beast's cold, unfeeling eyes and began shivering and shaking all over.

Bite bared his tearing teeth, then extended his tongue and licked the skin of her cheek, as if relishing the taste of the meal to come.

Now Lorna screamed and screamed with all her might.

'MUMMY! DADDY! HELP ME! HELLLLP MEEEEE!'

But her mummy and daddy weren't there.

Although terrified himself, brave little Tommy Tremar picked up a spade and ran towards the trog with the weapon raised above his head.

'Leave her alone, you big bully,' he shouted, as he bashed the flat of the spade down on the trog's foot.

'Trroggaaaaarrrhhhhh!' The trog roared as it swatted him away.

Tommy let go of the spade as he was thrown through the air like a rag doll, crashing into the huddle of children at the back of the shed.

Bite focused his attention on little Lorna once more.

'Mummy! Daddy! Mummy! Daddy!' She was still screaming and screaming for help.

'Trroggaaaaarrrhhhhh!' The trog picked up the spade, before taking a step backwards through the door of the shed and dropping the tiny girl to the ground, using its huge frame to cover the doorway to stop the other children escaping.

Even the youngest of the children knew that the monster planned to eat them one by one.

'Trroggaaaaarrrhhhhh!'

Bite then roared again as he raised the sharp spade above his head, preparing to slice little Lorna into manageable chunks.

Fluttafluttaflutta. Fluttafluttaflutta. Fluttafluttaflutta.

Just at that moment, from the direction of the forest that lined the perimeter of the playground, the children heard a familiar fluttering sound in the air, which very quickly got louder, and louder, and LOUDER.

Bite turned his hairy head to see what was making the noise… then roared his displeasure.

'Trroggaaarrhhhh!'

TWENTY-SEVEN

The Great Simoom at Camp Oasis

The sandstorm was gusting much harder when Louis arrived at Camp Oasis.

'The Great Simoom can blow for a week or more,' said Akbar Sharif as the sand spattered Louis' face, forcing him to close his eyes. 'We always keep enough provisions to survive for a month, just in case we are confined to our tents by such a storm.' With that, the sheik clapped his hands and gave orders. A desert meal was soon prepared.

Louis sat next to Akbar on a rug in a big tent and ate kebab and couscous, and bread and fruit, with all the desert riders, who had arranged themselves in a dining circle around the large bowls and platters of food.

Eating, like everyone else, with his fingers, Louis then washed it all down with a glass of fresh milk. He liked the taste of the milk a lot but, if he'd known it came from a goat, he might not have even tried it.

After the meal, Louis showed Akbar his Kernow Catapult and his Kaski. Then he removed *Zoomer* from its case and explained how it worked with *Rescuer*.

'Very ingenious,' said Akbar. 'I wonder, with all the troubles you have told me about in Kernowland, whether *Rescuer* will still be keeping watch on *The Revenger*.'

Louis hadn't thought of this and started to worry that *Zoomer* might have stopped working. He touched his finger on the map.

To his great joy, as he zoomed in, *The Revenger* suddenly came into view.

'Still working!' exclaimed Akbar. 'The pirates are certainly heading in the direction of Jungleland. And, as I imagined, the whalehorses are helping the ship make good time.'

'Can we go to Jungleland tomorrow?' asked Louis.

'I'm afraid that will not be possible,' answered Akbar, as the sides of the tent flapped with the force of the howling wind outside. 'The Great Simoom will certainly blow for a few more days. Long distance travel in the desert will not be possible until it stops. But do not concern yourself unduly, Prince Louis; your sister is still some way from Jungleland and it will be many moons before she arrives there. We will set off as soon as we can. And I am sure that – by the Will and Grace of Omni – everything will happen in the right way and at the right time.'

Louis hoped that Akbar was right.

TWENTY-EIGHT

Tintagel and the Tiny Tits

Fluttafluttaflutta. Fluttafluttaflutta. Fluttafluttaflutta.

The tiny tits, all following their leader, Tintagel, on a flight above the forest that bordered the school fence, had heard the little Kernowkids screaming from some way away.

They were now flying as fast as they could to help their friends.

The tiny birds loved the little Kernowkids because, with their teacher, Miss Perfect, the children had constructed a dozen bird tables in the school playground, and had put lots of food – such as seeds and nuts and bits of bread – out on the tables every day, with extra when it was cold.

Now it was the turn of the birds to help the Kernowkids.

The tiny tits were very small but they could attack their enemies in fighting flocks of hundreds. Working together as a team, a fighting flock was a formidable foe. They all had tiny but very sharp beaks. Each member of the flock could fly very fast, and they could all change direction at the same time, as if every individual immediately knew what all the others were thinking.

Tintagel quickly spied their hairy quarry in the doorway of the shed. Following their leader, the fearless fighting flock dived at the trog in spearhead formation. It was an awesome sight as five hundred diving birds reached a speed of a hundred kiloms per hour on their approach.

'Trroggaaarrhhhh!'

As they reached the trog, he roared and tried to swing the

spade at them. But the tiny tits were far too quick for the lumbering beast and they nipped Bite with pecking pinches all over his body.

'Trroggaaarrhhhh!' roared the trog again as he dropped the spade and waved his arms about, desperately trying to protect himself from the painful pinches. But the huge trog had no answer to the airborne onslaught. The tiny tits pecked him mercilessly, until he ran out of the playground and back down the road to Blystra Cliffs, roaring furiously as he went.

'Trroggaaarrhhhh!

'Trroggaaarrhhhh!

'Trroggaaarrhhhh!'

Fluttafluttaflutta. Peckpeckpeck. Fluttafluttaflutta. Peckpeckpeck.

Whilst half their number pecked at Bite's ears and neck and other places on his body as he stumbled back down the road towards Blystra Cliffs, the other half of the flock flew up into the air again to regroup.

This second group then launched another diving attack, now aiming straight for the beast's big hairy backside. Two hundred and fifty pinching beaks arrived at once on the trog's bottom, just as the monster had made it to the cliff edge.

'Trroggaaarrhhhh!'

The surprise and pain of this mass attack on his rear-end was enough to make Bite run straight over the edge.

'Trroggaaaaaaaaaaaaaaaaaaaaaaaaaaaaaaaaaarrrhhhhh!'

The monster roared a very long roar as he plunged towards the rocks below, with the tiny tits still pecking incessantly at his bottom all the way down. Just before the trog hit the rocks with a crunch, the fighting flock all stopped the bottom-pecking and flew straight up, high into the sky.

Here, they regrouped, before flying rapidly back to the playground, where the other children were comforting Lorna Luckett.

Tintagel flew to Tommy Tremar and hovered in front of his face.

'I think he wants us to follow him,' said Tommy to the others. Tintagel performed a body-nod to show Tommy that he was right.

So, whilst most of the tiny tits flew over the school roof and off into the distance, the Kernowkids followed Tintagel and a small squadron of his friends into the woods.

TWENTY-NINE

Trog Feast

Meanwhile, the other four trogs had stomped up the beach and climbed to the clifftop. They were now trying to decide which direction along the road to take – town or school.

One of their number, Munch, caught the scent of the Kernowkids and set off up the hill towards the school in search of childmeat.

The remaining three trogs saw smoke rising from the town and decided to go that way. They were so hungry after two weeks of no food that none of them was bothered whether they ate young and tender flesh or old and tough flesh.

As they made their way into the burning, smoking town, the trogs all roared to announce their arrival.

'Trroggaaarrrhhh!' 'Trroggaaarrrhhh!' 'Trroggaaarrrhhh!'

The only people left in Towan Blystra were the older people; the grannies and granddads who were no longer members of the defence forces and so had not gone off to fight The Invader. Those who had survived the bombing were helping to rescue those less fortunate than themselves.

Suddenly, one of the granddads spotted the three monsters. He pointed a quivering finger towards the cliff end of Fore Street.

'T-T-TROGS! H-H-HIDE!'

But it was too late. The three trogs fell on the old people, scratching and tearing, and biting and chewing.

The trog feast had begun.

THIRTY

Munch

When Munch entered the school playground, he followed his nose. But he found the shed empty… his prey had gone. The hungry trog sniffed the ground for fresh tracks and soon discovered that a group of Kernowkids had headed into the woods.

Munch again had two options: follow the scent into the trees or go into town and share the older, tougher meat with the other trogs. It was no contest. The smell of Kernowkid was simply too tempting to ignore, and the monster was soon hot on the trail of Tommy Tremar and his friends.

'Trroggaaarrrhhhhh!'

In the woods, the Kernowkids heard the trogroar in the distance as they ran.

'Run faster!' shouted Tommy, who seemed to have become the leader.

'TROGGAAARRRHHHHH!'

The roar was getting louder… the huge hungry hairy beast was gaining fast.

Fluttafluttaflutta.

Tommy was dismayed to see Tintagel and his friends fly away as the trog got nearer.

Why have they left us now? he wondered.

A few minutes later, Munch caught up with the Kernowkids as they came to a big pond. The only way forward was into the water.

But, none of them could swim very well and the other side of the pond seemed so far away.

And the only way back was *through* the trog… not a tempting option.

'We're trapped,' whimpered little Lorna, now quivering with fear as she watched a long bead of saliva dripping from the side of the trog's frothing mouth.

Munch searched along the buffet of Kernowkids with his cold, hungry eyes, as if finding it hard to choose his starter.

The Kernowkids cowered in a huddle, wondering which of them would be first.

THIRTY-ONE

Howl

'Howwwwllllll.'

As the Kernowkids waited for the trog to choose one of them to eat, there was the unmistakeable howl of a wolf near by.

Paddapadda. Herfherfherf. Next came the sound of lots of padding little paws and a great deal of heavy panting.

Fluttafluttaflutta. Then the familiar sound of Tintagel and the small squadron of tiny tits.

'Woof! Woof! Woof!'

Next moment, a pack of seven yapping hounds – with big floppy ears, short legs, and long brown bodies – appeared in the clearing as if from nowhere, led towards the trog by Tintagel and his friends.

'Sausagedogs!' exclaimed Lorna in surprise.

Two of the hounds carried each end of a rope made of entwined vines in their jaws. They ran either side of the trog and then around and around him at lightning speed.

'Trroggaaarrrhhhhh!' Before he knew it, Munch's legs were tied tightly. He roared in anger as he tore at the vinerope with one of his clawpaws whilst swinging his club wildly in an attempt to bash the little dogs with it.

As Munch struggled, one of the hounds ran along a fallen tree trunk and sprang off the end of it. To the Kernowkids, it looked like the dog was flying!

The soaring hound clamped its jaw around the clawpaw holding the club and hung on doggedly as Munch roared in pain and swirled his arm around, first this way and then that, in a desperate attempt to rid himself of the unwelcome appendage.

'Trroggaaarrrhhhhh!'

Another hound chewed a couple of Munch's toes.

'Trroggaaarrrhhhhh!'

Another bit his ankle.

'Trroggaaarrrhhhhh!'

Another leapt from the ground and gripped the inside of his thigh with its teeth. This was certainly the most painful bite so far, and the trog bent at the knee, struggling to maintain its balance.

'HOWWWWLLLLL!'

Just as Munch was falling backwards, a giant wolf raced out of the trees, sprang up on its hind legs and sank its sharp canine teeth deep into the trog's hairy throat.

'Trroggaa…' Munch tried to roar, but could only manage a feeble gurgle.

The huge trog continued to fall backwards with the giant wolf still gripping his throat… he was dead before he hit the ground.

'Howwwwwwwwwwwwwwwwwwwwwwwwwwlllll.'

Howl, the Great Wolf, stood on the chest of his kill and howled triumphantly.

At that moment, a heavily pregnant hound padded slowly out of the trees to congratulate her mate and her seven children on their victory.

Dribble's three brothers and four sisters gathered lovingly around their mother, Dearest, as she made her way forward.

THIRTY-TWO

Cule Fights Back

Cule was the junior cliff climbing champion of Kernowland and he held the record for scaling the High Cliff faster than anyone. In no time at all, he had reached the top; where he was greeted by the terrible sight of his home town in flames.

Cule ran as fast as he could go.

'Aaarrrrrrrrghh! Nohhhhhh!'

As he got nearer, he heard the cries and screams of the grannies and granddads as the trogs rounded them up. It was an awful sound.

When he got to the town square, he peered from behind a wall to see what the trogs were doing. They had made a makeshift trogtrough of the fountain in the middle of the square, and were depositing the old folk in there. They were obviously planning a very big feast.

Cule hid behind walls and ran through back gardens as he made his way home. He hoped upon hope that Gran had escaped. His parents had died a long time ago in an accident at sea, and Gran had brought him up from the time when he was only a baby. He loved her very much.

When he got home, he ran around the back, scaled the garden wall and quietly opened the back door. To his horror, there was Gran's blood-stained apron, lying by the hearth where she had been cooking pastys. It was torn to shreds.

Cule stood and stared in a mixture of shock, sadness, and anger.

'Trroggaaarrrhhhhh!'

The young man spun around to see a nine-foot trog behind him. Under the low ceiling, the salivating beast was bent over with its arms outstretched. It lunged forward, trying to grab him with its long sharp claws.

Luckily, Cule was the champion junior gymnast of Kernowland, and he immediately executed a back flip out of the way. Then, in one swift and flowing movement, as the trog lunged again, Cule grabbed up a sharp kitchen knife, leapt onto the table… and sank the long blade deep into the monster's neck.

'Trroggaaarrrhhhhh!' The wounded creature roared as it fell backwards, and landed with a thud on the cold stone slabs of the kitchen floor.

After making sure he had killed the trog, Cule raced upstairs to his bedroom. From under the bed, he pulled out a large trunk.

Inside the trunk were the weapons he had learned to use during training exercises for the time he could join the Land Guardians, when he came of age on his eighteenth birthday... which happened to be that very day.

He took out his Kernow Catapult, Kernow Crossbow, and Kernbow, as well as the ammo belts and quivers for each weapon. He strapped on his sword, longdagger, and Kaski.

Descending the stairs, Cule then went to a drawer, took out a key and opened a locked cabinet on the wall. Inside the cabinet were two ancient pistols, a musket, and a Kernowaxe. They had belonged to his father, who had been a brave captain of the Land Guardians.

Now heavily armed, the young warrior marched briskly into the town square, where the two remaining trogs were still piling their victims into the fountain trogtrough.

'Hey, trogs,' he shouted at the top of his voice, 'why don't you pick on someone who can fight back?!'

The trogs stared at their challenger in disbelief. They were two nine-foot trogs. He was a scrawny youth. Was he stupid?

'Trroggaaarrrhhhhh!'

'Trroggaaarrrhhhhh!'

The two trogs roared and raised their clubs as they pounded across the square towards their youthful adversary.

Cule was taken by surprise when one of them hurled its club straight at him. With little time to react, he felt the full force of the club as it hit him on the thigh, numbing his whole leg. Falling to one knee as the two hairy beasts broke into a sprint, he reached for his pistols and unleashed both barrels into the trog that had thrown the club.

But the trog just absorbed the shots… and kept on coming.

With only seconds until they would be upon him, Cule unquivered and fired off an arrow from his Kernbow. The arrow struck home, right through the chest of the trog he had shot moments earlier. The force of the arrow carried the trog four paces backwards before it fell to the ground.

'Trroggaaarrrhhhhh!'

The other trog was only paces away, with its club raised high in readiness for attack.

Now recovered enough from the stun to his leg, Cule stood up and hopped towards a garden wall before throwing himself over it, in a desperate attempt to put something solid between him and his hairy attacker.

Not the brainiest of beasts, the trog seemed momentarily confused by this manoeuvre, but it was soon advancing towards the wall.

Cule bent down low and moved along the wall to the corner of the garden. As the trog jumped over the wall, at the place it was expecting Cule to be, the champion marksman was able to fire a crossbow bolt into its side, followed by a round from the musket. The trog fell sideways.

Cule seized his chance, drew his sword and ran at the dazed beast as fast as his numb leg would allow. He plunged the sword into his foe, time after time… until he was sure it was dead.

'And that's for GRAN!' he declared on the last blow.

THIRTY-THREE

Invasion From The West

The Seven Mermaids of Wra were merrily swimming in the waters a little off the coast of Land's End. They had no idea that today was Darkness Day.

Megan was the first of the fishmaidens to spot the invaders. As she flipped out of the water, and splashed back down in play, she saw the Viking longships on the horizon, where the sea met the sky to the west of Kernowland.

'We must warn the Kernowfolk right away,' said Megan to her friends. 'We'd better split up. Tell the first Kernowlander you see that there are longships approaching from the West.

'Go now! Swim as fast as you can.'

The mermaids all swam off in different directions to raise the alarm.

* * *

Hrappr Bloodaxe stood on the deck of his longship, *The Pillager*. The vessel had round shields all along the port and starboard sides, and a carved statue of the wargoddess, *Thora*, above the curved bow.

Hrappr wore a helmet with four horns sticking out of it, one at the front, one at the back, and one on either side. He was the leader of the Vikings of Kramned, and it was his job to attack Kernowland from the West.

The Viking leader had a special interest in the invasion; he was looking forward to his marriage to the beautiful Princess Kea, just as Manaccan had promised.

The Vikings were men of incredible size. The smallest of them was twice the size of most Kernish soldiers.

'Vaarrrrr!' The largest of all the Vikings was Vik, who stood next to his leader laughing loudly as he waved his sword in the air. Like all the other Vikings, Vik also had his big double-headed waraxe securely stuck in his belt. Vik was really looking forward to the battle.

'Well, my leader,' he said to Hrappr, 'we'll soon be chopping off heads in Kernowland.'

'Vaarrrrr!' Hrappr roared in agreement as he looked around to make sure that all the other fifty-four longships were keeping up.

Hrappr's longship was longer than the others… it had one hundred oars on either side. This was for a good reason; it was pulling a large tentraft – attached to the ship by thick strong ropes – in which there was something *very* big and *very* heavy.

Whooooshh! Splashh!

Suddenly, a set of reindeer antlers flew though the air out of the open flap of the canvas tent and landed with a splash in the sea.

Whooooshh! Splashh!

Another set of antlers quickly followed the first. Whatever was in the tentraft… was devouring whole reindeers!

The Vikings had picked up two other armies on their journey to Kernowland: the Highland Tocs of Tocsland, and the Eriemen of Erieland. Their leaders stood alongside Hrappr at the bow of his longship.

Murdo was the Clanchief of a fierce clan of Highland Tocs: the McStabbers. His sister, Murda, was his second-in-command.

Although Murdo was a huge and very hairy man, his sister was even bigger and hairier than him.

Murda McStabber had won the Highland Games against all the men every year since she had first entered at the age of fourteen. She held every one of the all-time records for caber tossing, stone lifting, and hammer throwing. She was a formidable warrior, and her brother was very proud of her.

Murdo McStabber had a special interest in the invasion; he was looking forward to his marriage to the beautiful Princess Kea, just as Manaccan had promised.

Shawn O'Shorne was the Chieftain of the Eriemen. He was a short man, something he seemed to be making up for every time he spoke because he shouted every word at the top of his voice. For this reason, he was known everywhere as 'Shouting Shawn'.

He didn't like boats and had spent the entire journey being sick – and generally feeling queasy. He couldn't wait to get his feet back on dry land.

Shawn had a special interest in the invasion; he was looking forward to his marriage to the beautiful Princess Kea, just as Manaccan had promised.

The Chieftain of the Eriemen had a leprechaun to help protect and advise him. Although they were all nasty, vindictive creatures, this leprechaun was the most loathsome of its kind. It sat in a special saddle on Shawn's shoulder, whispering vile verses in his ear, telling its master all sorts of nasty things he could do.

The loathsome leprechaun's name was *Limerick*.

Like all leprechauns, Limerick had a very flexible neck. He could stretch it up and spin his head almost in a complete circle. This allowed him to watch out for Shawn's back. The leprechaun had cross-eyes, which rolled around and around – often in opposite directions – whenever he became excited or angry. Nevertheless, his eyesight was exceedingly keen.

As Shawn stood next to Hrappr, Limerick suddenly stood up in the shoulder saddle, straining to see something as he held on to Shawn's ear for balance.

The leprechaun began rolling his eyes. Then he spun his head around in a circle and back again, before shouting a vile verse at the top of his voice, as he bounced up and down excitedly in the shoulder saddle…

> *Merry Mermaids do I spy*
> *With my rolling Leprechaun eye*
> *Telling tales they soon will try*
> *Methinks it's time they all should DIE!*

Everyone at the bow heard what Limerick said he had seen.

'We must stop them,' boomed Hrappr.

'Odium, we need you up here... and bring the turning twigs.'

THIRTY-FOUR

Prince Louis... THIEF!

Sheviok Scurvy was looking through the small window in the guardroom, smirking gleefully at the dark cloud above the castle.

'Looks like the Forcesphere destruction plan has worked,' he said to his co-conspirators. 'Won't be long now and they'll be letting us out of here for our rewards.'

'Do you think the Young Master will be cross that we haven't got the spare Golden Key, Mr Scurvy?' asked Mrs Maggitt, as if she were really rather worried about it. 'After all, you did say he was very keen to have it.'

'He's not the Young Master anymore, Madam Maggitt,' said Scurvy. 'The guard told me that he's already become King. As for the key, we'll just tell *King* Manaccan what happened. The boy stole the key; it's as simple as that. We didn't lose it; it was stolen by that little thief! As long as we all say the same thing, everything will be fine. They'll be after the prince for the key.'

'Yes, we'll all say the same thing… got that?' reiterated Mr Maggitt, glaring at his wife to try to make sure she understood.

'I think it's best if you do the talking, Mr Scurvy' said Mrs Maggitt nervously. 'All this excitement is making me feel quite faint and I might just say something wrong.'

At that moment, a troop of soldiers arrived outside the cell.

A corporal spoke to the guard. 'I am to escort the prisoners for an audience with King Manaccan. Apparently there has been some mistake and they are innocent of all charges.'

THIRTY-FIVE

Invasion From The South

The Moors, Gauls, and Guerreros formed the armada attacking Kernowland from the South.

Ali Blabla was the leader of the Moors of Occorom. His second-in-command, the wurld-renowned warrior, Saracen, towered over him as they stood, side by side, on the Moor flagship: *Al-Rabat*.

There were sixty-six Moor Dhows in the invasion fleet. They had huge blades on the front which curved around the bows, just above the waterline, so that they could slash into enemy ships.

Twenty-four of the dhows were special 'bird carriers'. They carried gigantic vulturerats, which were resting on the decks in preparation for their revolting task of picking the corpses clean of flesh after the battle for Kernowland.

All the Moors had beards and wore head scarves and long flowing djellabarobes. Dangling from each of their sash belts was a scything scimitar in a decorated scabbard. The scimitars had two-handed handles to make it easier to slash with them. In the hands of a Moor warrior, the long-handled scything scimitar could cut through the flesh of enemies like a hot knife through butter.

The Moors rode into battle on chargercamels, which were racers, specially trained for close-quarter combat. On the dhows, the animals shared the living and sleeping quarters with their riders, so it was all a bit cramped on board; and a little smelly too.

The Moors brought with them a terrible weapon of weather warfare… thunderbolt clouds. As the two dark clouds floated ominously above the dhows, lightning flashed within them and a dull, rumbling thunder accompanied the fleet as it sailed onwards.

Sitting on the bow of his dhow, Ali Blabla was smiling broadly because he had a special interest in the invasion. He was looking forward to his marriage to the beautiful Princess Kea, just as Manaccan had promised.

Gerard de Gall – known as 'Garlic' by those who had smelt his bad breath – was the leader of the ghastly Gauls of Ecnarf.

Gerard was a dashing, good-looking, and clever knight. Or rather, that's what he liked to tell everybody. He was really very ugly and very stupid, with truly horrendous halitosis, but nobody wanted to tell him because he was such a good fighter and would kill you as soon as look at you. Gerard stared at his ugly face in the little mirror that he carried everywhere. It was the tenth time he had studied himself that morning!

'Garlic' de Gall had a special interest in the invasion. He was looking forward to his marriage to the beautiful Princess Kea, just as Manaccan had promised.

There were seventy-seven Gaul galleons in the invasion fleet. They were especially effective in battle because they were pulled by whalehorsepower.

The galleons of Ecnarf were accompanied by hundreds of black, sleek, shiny creatures with long dorsal fins that protruded above the water as they swam alongside the warships. They were giant sawtooth sharks… mutants specially trained for battle against the famous dolphineers of Kernowland.

El Toro de Torremolinos was the leader of the Guerreros, who came from the land of Niaps. His second-in-command was Gordo

La Grande, a very fat warrior who was constantly eating from a bag full of food that hung from his belt.

El Toro had a special interest in the invasion. He was looking forward to his marriage to the beautiful Princess Kea, just as Manaccan had promised.

Eight of the eighty-eight Guerrero galleons were much bigger than the others, because they had to accommodate a living cargo: battlebulls.

El Toro's battlebulls were the biggest bulls in the wurld, bred specially for combat by the mutationeers of Niaps. They were fifteen feet long and had horns that stretched six feet from end to end. The points of the horns were tipped with steel, and were sharpened daily. The bulls were completely black, apart from their horns, and their hooves, and their fiery red eyes.

El Toro and his Guerreros rode into battle on their huge black bulls. The Guerreros and the battlebulls were feared throughout the empire. And with very good reason... no army had ever defeated them. It was now widely believed that they were invincible.

They were heading for a battle with the famous donkeyteers of Kernowland.

THIRTY-SIX

The Stolen Key

At the end of his story, Misty said to Clevercloggs: '*And I'm trying to find out what happened to my friend Prince Louis, who is a good boy and a brave young warrior. The last I knew, he was heading for Kernow Castle.*'

'Well, that certainly is an interesting tale,' said Clevercloggs, scratching his chin as he put Misty into the front pocket of his dungarees along with the spare key. 'Now, you mentioned Drym, and Scurvy, and Mr and Mrs Maggitt; I'm sure they're all in this book that Dribble gave me.'

Misty watched from the pocket, and Mr Bude listened from the front of the cart, as the clever gnome turned the pages of the diary as he spoke. He stopped at a particular page and pointed.

ESZN
NBHHJUU
NBHHJUU
TDVSWZ
XFOESPO
XBSMFHHBO

'Yes, here it is... **ESZN**, that decodes to *DRYM*; **NBHHJUU**, twice, that's *MAGGITT* and *MAGGITT*; and **TDVSWZ**, that's *SCURVY*.

'Drym was with Wendron and Warleggan when we saw them

and they're both on this list in the diary too. So you can be pretty sure they're all in it together.

'Now, the heading at the top of the page in the diary decodes to *THE TEN*, so there are at least four other traitors we must find out about, but, as we can see, the other names are all smudged.

'The conspirators must have stolen the spare Golden Key from Goonhilly, although I'm not sure how they did it, as it's closely guarded. Perhaps one of the traitors works there. I'd imagine they wanted the key to gain access to the Golden Cavern and the Crystal Door. All part of their treacherous plotting, no doubt.'

'I think, under the circumstances, that you'd better hide under the compost,' said Mr Bude to Clevercloggs, 'just in case Wendron and her cronies are flying around in the Skycycle looking for you.'

'My thoughts precisely,' agreed Clevercloggs as he covered himself with lumps of the smelly compost and strands of straw so that he couldn't be seen from above.

As they rattled along in the cart, Misty was certainly very glad that they were making for Kernow Castle, because that was where Louis and Mr Sand had been heading before all the excitement with Monstro, the Brazilian brain-boiler tree, in the Carnivore Cage.

He hoped and hoped and hoped that Louis had made it to the castle safely.

THIRTY-SEVEN

Invasion From The East

Angar Saxxon, who was known better as 'Angar the Angry', was the leader of the Angles of Angleland. By special concession, which he gave now and then, the name 'Angleland' had not been turned backwards by Evile. The country of the Angles was to the east of Kernowland, the two kingdoms being separated by the River Tamar. The river's passage marked most of the border so that, apart from six miles of marshy ground in the north, Kernowland was almost an island surrounded by water.

Angar had a special interest in the invasion; he was looking forward to his marriage to the beautiful Princess Kea, just as Manaccan had promised.

The Angle general sat proudly on Hisser, his huge brown heavyhorse, and surveyed his army of ten thousand footsoldiers and three thousand cavalrymen. His orders were to attack the half of the Great Wall of Kernow that lay to the north of Launceston Gate, the only entrance along the whole wall.

Angar's artillery consisted of sixty-six carnage cannon, built specifically for the purpose of knocking down battlements from a distance. Their range was about one kilom and each required ten cannoneers to operate it. On Angar's command, all the carnage cannon had been rolled into position as soon as he had received word that the dark mushroom cloud had risen above Truro Castle. The iron tubes of destruction now stretched at regular intervals on the hills within range of The Wall.

One cannon was far longer and heavier than all the others. It even had a name: *Bombardum*. The long barrel of this great gun alone weighed fifty evtons, and it needed twenty large shire horses to pull it. Bombardum was positioned to the south of all the other guns, on a hill right opposite Launceston Gate.

Meanwhile, the Zulus and their Animal Army of Acirfa were massing in readiness for an attack on the southern stretch of the Great Wall.

Generalchief Shakabantu had a special interest in the invasion; he was looking forward to his marriage to the beautiful Princess Kea, just as Manaccan had promised.

Shakabantu was preparing to send in his heavy armour… gigantic rhinophants. Each a living, breathing, battering ram weighing thirty evtons, rhinophants were part rhino, part elephant, specifically grown by the mutationeers of Acirfa to attack fortifications. Their hides were as thick and strong as armour plate. They had both rhino horns and elephant tusks.

Every rhinophant had a saddlebox on its back. Each saddlebox carried a dozen Zulus armed with bows, spears, and shields.

Behind the rhinophants were arrayed the forces of the Animal Army: thousands of roaring, screeching, scratching, mutant beasts.

And, flexing their webby wings in readiness for the attack, were more than three hundred giant bloodguzzling hairybats, each capable of sucking all the blood from human-sized prey in less than a minute.

Every flesh-eating member of the Animal Army – which was most of them – had been promised they could eat one adult or two children in Kernowland when the battle was over. They were all drooling in anticipation because, like the trogs, they had been starved for two weeks in preparation for Darkness Day.

THIRTY-EIGHT

Prince Louis... MURDERER!

Misty listened to the wheels of the old cart squeaking along the road as he worried whether he would ever see Louis again.

Mr Bude was worried about the dark mushroom cloud still hanging ominously over the castle. It created a shadow on the ground which spread out in all directions from the Dome Tower.

As they passed under the shadow at the edge of the cloud, Clevercloggs was deep in thought.

On their arrival at the castle, they were halted by the guard at the gate.

'What has happened here?' asked Mr Bude.

'The King's cousin, Prince Louis, did it,' began the guard, 'he blew up the Forcesphere.'

'But how?' asked Mr Bude.

'Apparently took exploding cataballs into the White Light Ceremony and murdered the King and the Queen. He also killed the guards, and the Rainbow Wizards, nearly everyone who was in the Prism Chamber. I heard that Princelord Manaccan, Wizard Violothan, and Dr Lizard were lucky to survive.'

'Well I never, dear oh dear,' said Mr Bude.

'From what they're saying, it looks like Princess Kea was the one behind it,' continued the guard. 'Wanted the throne before her time. And, as well as that treacherous Prince Louis, can you believe that her other accomplices were Mr Sand and Professor Mullion?'

'Well I never, what a carry-on,' said Mr Bude.

'Sand, the professor, and the princess are in the dungeons,' added the guard. 'But Prince Louis escaped. There's a warrant out for the arrest of Clevercloggs the gnome as well. Apparently he was one of the conspirators.'

'And do they know where that young scoundrel, Prince Louis, has gone?' questioned Mr Bude.

PRINCE LOUIS
OF FORESTLAND
MURDERER!
WANTED DEAD OR ALIVE,
PREFERABLY DEAD!

'No. Just disappeared into thin air, they say. He must be on the run, far away by now. We're putting up these posters to try to apprehend him. Little *murderer*. I know what I'd do if I caught up with him.'

Misty looked through a crack in the side of the cart at the poster the guard was pointing to. It had a likeness of Louis drawn on it, and there were words below the picture.

'Well I never, dear oh dear,' sighed Mr Bude again, as if the news was a great deal of alarming information to take in at once. 'I suppose that means Princelord Manaccan will have to become King.'

'Already is,' explained the guard. 'They've not had an official coronation yet, but he's the new King all right. There's no time for any ceremonies though; there's an emergency on. The traitorous little prince also blew up the Forcesphere, making way for an invasion. The flameflares have gone up and the pigeons have been bringing in terrible reports from the coast.'

'We'd better arm ourselves then,' said Mr Bude, patriotically.

'Might not need to,' continued the guard. 'King Manaccan says that, without the Forcesphere to defend us, resistance is futile. He's told the Parliament of Bards that he wants to negotiate with Evile.'

'Well I never,' repeated Mr Bude. 'Well I never.'

From his hiding place under the smelly compost, Clevercloggs had listened to everything. He was fuming that innocent people were being blamed whilst the real traitors were getting away with it.

It just wasn't FAIR!

Although he had to stay quiet for the moment, it was very clear that something would *have* to be done to right these wrongs.

A clever plan was forming in his mind.

THIRTY-NINE

Get The Mermaids!

Odium the Odious joined Hrappr Bloodaxe, Shawn O'Shorne, and Murdo McStabber at the bow of *The Pillager*. He was the dark magician of the Vikings and wore a long dull-grey robe.

Odium took two small 'turning twigs' from a pouch. The magical twigs were so called because they could be turned into other things. Holding one twig in each palm, the dark magician began to cast a very short spellverse…

> *Turning twigs*
> *On these palms laid*
> *Turn into*
> *Mini-mermaids*

With that, each of the twigs turned into a tiny mermaid. The two little fishmaidens squirmed about in the dark magician's palms.

Shawn, Murdo, and the Viking warriors, watched in awe as Odium handed the mini-mermaids over to Hrappr Bloodaxe.

'Summon the killerwhales,' ordered Hrappr.

With that, one of the Vikings sounded a horn, and two huge black and white beasts, Kracka and Kruncha, came alongside the boat.

Hrappr threw one of the mini-mermaids to Kruncha who caught it in his teeth and gulped it down. Then it was Kracka's turn for a snack.

Having given the killerwhales the scent and taste of their prey, Hrappr then pointed to the seven tails that were fanning out in all directions in the distance, desperately swimming to raise the alarm.

'There's your breakfast, my hungry ones. Get the mermaids!'

Kracker and Kruncha didn't need telling twice. They set off at great speed in pursuit of a mermaid meal.

'DRUMMER!' bawled Hrapper, 'sound the War Drum.'

Pum... Pum... Pum... Pum.

The drum pounded out the beat for the rowing stroke.

The Vikings were now crazy with bloodlust.

'Get... The... Mer... Maids..., Get... The... Mer... Maids...,' they chanted at the top of their voices, as they rowed in time with the pum pum of the War Drum. As the drum beat faster and faster, the Vikings chanted and rowed faster and faster.

'Get... The... Mer... Maids..., Get... The... Mer... Maids...'

The waves lashed past the sides of the boat as *The Pillager* began to go at an incredible speed in pursuit of the mermaids.

The two killerwhales had soon rounded up the seven mermaids as if they were dogs herding a flock of sheep. The frightened fishmaidens had been corralled into a small inlet on the coast of Land's End.

Kracka and Kruncha were very pleased with themselves and very much looking forward to their mermaid meal. However, even though they were extremely hungry, the two whales were so well trained by their master that they waited in the mouth of the inlet for his instruction to move in for the kill.

As Hrappr's longboat soon reached the inlet mouth, he held his waraxe above his head and yelled at the top of his voice.

'Devour them!'

Needing no further encouragement, the two sea carnivores moved slowly in for their feast.

Then, just as the killerwhales were upon them, the mermaids suddenly disappeared underwater, diving as deep as they could go, desperately seeking a means of escape.

Kracka and Kruncha dived after them, making a big splash in the water as they went.

'Vaarrrrr!' Hrappr and the other Vikings cheered in anticipation of the whales surfacing with mermaid's tails between their teeth.

However, by an enormous stroke of luck, the mermaids spied an undersea cave in this inlet, whose entrance was just big enough for them to squeeze through. The mermaids headed straight for the cave and each of them swam through the small hole in the rocks as fast as they could go.

And they all made it through in time... except Megan, who was bringing up the rear.

CRUUUUNCH!

Just as Megan was swimming through the hole to safety, Kruncha chased fast and crunched his two rows of sharp teeth down on her tail, biting it clean off.

Inside the cave, one by one, the mermaids surfaced in a little cavepool and hauled themselves onto the rocky floor. Mylene counted as each of her friends reached safety.

'One, two, three, four, five, six.'

Morwenna was first to voice her concern.

'Where's Megan?'

FORTY

Pemberley's Peepholes

Pemberley the butler had found it difficult to believe that Mr Sand and Professor Mullion were traitors. He had found it even harder to believe that the lovely Princess Kea and little Prince Louis could have killed the King and Queen. And, as for Clevercloggs, he was *absolutely certain* that the wise old gnome of Washaway Wood was loyal to Kernowland with every bone in his little body.

Pemberley may have been a bit 'stiff and starchy' on the outside, but he was really a brave freedom fighter; a secret member of RAE, helping King Kernow in the wurldwide underground fight against Evile's Empire.

So, ever since he had heard the announcement by Princelord – now King! – Manaccan, Chief Wizard Violothan, and Dr Lizard that these good and loyal people were traitors and murderers, Pemberley had been suspicious of the messengers. He was determined to discover more.

Pemberley's father, and his father's father before him – and his great grandfathers as far back as anyone could remember – had all been butlers to the Royal Family of Kernowland. So, Pemberley had been born at the castle, and, as a boy, had spent many an hour exploring its network of secret tunnels, corridors, panels, and doors that very few people knew about.

He was now spying through one of his secret peepholes – the one behind the removable eye on the portrait of King Kernow XXXIII in the Throne Room. The butler watched, hoping for clues, as the new monarch greeted Wendron, Warleggan, and Drym when they entered the Throne Room.

'Aahhhhh, my good friends, welcome… that makes nine of us here,' he gushed, as he sat – rather too smugly in Pemberley's opinion – on the Grand Throne of Kernowland.

Peering through his tiny peephole, the butler saw that there were nine chairs arranged in a line on the red carpet, all facing the throne. The three recent arrivals took their seats, so that eight people now sat in a row in front of their new King.

Scanning the line-up, Pemberley was sure that such a motley collection of individuals must be up to no good.

At one end were Mawla Maggitt, Malpas Maggitt, and Sheviok Scurvy, who, for reasons unclear to Pemberley, had all been released from the Guard Room. Next in the line was Dr Lizard. In the middle, on the fifth chair, sat Violothan in his long violet robes with his hood covering his head as usual. Then came Miss Wendron, Squire Warleggan, and Melanchol Drym. There was one empty chair on the end.

'Only one to come and we can begin,' said King Manaccan. 'Do we know if Lister has been successful in his task?'

'It would appear so, Your Majesticness,' answered Dr Lizard, with a smirk that convinced Pemberley he was definitely a villain. 'We have received a pigeon with a note; Mr Lister has completed his task and should be here very soon.'

Before anyone could say anything further, the doors opened and a short, thin man with a twisted face entered. He wore round, metal-rimmed, pince-nez spectacles, which were balanced on the bridge of his hooked nose. As he approached, he hunched his shoulders and rubbed his hands together, whilst listing the towns and villages in Kernowland in alphabetical order under his breath.

'Addington, Albaston, Allet, Altarnun, Amalebra, Amalveor, Anderton, Angarrack, Angarrick, Antony, Antony Passage, Ashill, Ashton, Badgall, Badharlick, Bake, Bakesdown, Baldhu, Ball…'

Lester Lister was Kernowland's Counterupper. The Office of the Counterupper was in Bodmin and Mr Lister was responsible for keeping lists of all the important things in the kingdom – such as who had to pay what in taxes, how many children were in each school and all their names, who did which job and for how long they had done it, who was married to whom, and so on.

Mr Lister was one of those people whose name matched his personality. Although everything was written down in special Listing Books, he loved to try to memorise things and he would recite the lists endlessly by mumbling them to himself.

Sometimes, when he was especially pleased because he had remembered a long list, he would start it again, but this time from the end, reciting the whole thing backwards. And, because he spoke very few words apart from his lists, Lester Lister was known to all around as… 'The Bodmin Bore'.

'I hear we must congratulate you, Mr Lister,' said King Manaccan. 'Assuming you can confirm that you've been successful in the abduction of Mullion's wife and three children, and that you've had them incarcerated in Bodmin Gaol.'

'I can indeed, sire,' answered Mr Lister. 'They came quietly when I told them we had the Professor here at the castle. I took great care to list all the things we would do to him if they didn't do as they were told.'

Dr Lizard punched the air. He simply could not conceal his delight.

'Fabulous work. The good professor will do everything we want him to do once he knows his family is held hostage in the gaol. We'll soon be able to offer the Emperor control of the eyes in the skies and zooming maps and everything else Mullion has invented. His Imperiousness will be very grateful and we'll all be handsomely rewarded, I'm sure.'

The line of traitors all nodded in agreement and congratulated themselves as Mr Lister took his seat at the end of the row.

They're working for the Emperor! Pemberley seethed at the treachery unfolding before his eyes as the King spoke again.

'Now, first things first. Mr Scurvy, I believe you have something for me?'

Scurvy squirmed in his seat. He hadn't been relishing the prospect of explaining the loss of the Golden Key to his leader. He knew that Manaccan wanted it to present as a gift to the Emperor on his triumphant entry into Kernowland after the invasion.

It was common knowledge that Evile loved receiving gifts from his subjects, and he especially coveted the Golden Key because he could use it to travel instantly to and from anywhere in Erthwurld through Godolphin's Crystal Door. It would make him even more powerful.

All ten traitors had agreed when they were plotting that it would be easier to steal the spare key from Goonhilly than the main one that King Kernow kept in a secret place; especially since they had Dr Lizard – 'the Insider' – on their side down at Kernowland's main science facility.

Scurvy shifted nervously on his chair as he tried to think how best to explain that Louis had stolen the spare key.

There were, of course, two things that he and the other traitors had no way of knowing: Louis no longer had the spare key but, rather, had been given King Kernow's key by Mr Sand… and it was Misty the little blue mouse who had the spare!

FORTY-ONE

Fire From The Sky

From his observation room at Pendennis Castle, Admiral Crumplehorn of the Kernish Navy could survey the whole of Falmouth Port.

As soon as he had seen and heard the invasion warnings, the Admiral had ordered his ships to sail.

The Kernish Navy was regarded as one of the best in the wurld, but few of the captains had had time to prepare for a battle, and most were unable to get underway before the Moors struck.

The Admiral watched in despair as the thunderbolt clouds floated into position above the port.

Boom! Boom!

The destructive forces within the clouds were set loose by igniter balls fired from cannon on board the invading dhows, which were still some way out to sea.

Clap! Sszzzzzz! Clap! Sszzzzzz!

Thunder clapped and lightning bolts zigzagged down from the clouds, setting fire to ships and buildings in the port.

CAABOOOOOOOOOOOOOOOM!

The Admiral flinched as his flaming armoury exploded.

However, despite the chaos and confusion, a few of Crumplehorn's ships had been able to get underway and, although hopelessly outnumbered, they bravely sailed towards The Invader.

The dolphineer units along the south coast of Kernowland,

being small and mobile, had reacted very quickly after the invasion warnings.

The squadrons which had been in Falmouth Port had swum out before the thunderbolt clouds arrived, and they now joined those from all the other southern bases.

Each dolphineer was heavily armed, not only with their crystal-tipped stingers, but also with explosive crystal mines and crystal grenades.

The dolphineers mustered alongside the few Kernish ships that had been able to set sail from the port, and – at a point some way to the north-west of Falmouth – made ready to do battle with the Gauls and their sawtooth sharks.

With Kernowland's Navy and the dolphineers otherwise engaged with the Moors and Gauls, El Toro's galleons met very little resistance as they sailed towards the coast of Kernowland.

This part of the invasion plan had worked well. The southern offensive had been so fast, and the numbers so overwhelming, that a gap had been created in Kernowland's defences.

El Toro was able to unload his men and supplies along the beaches to the north-west of Looe Island without significant challenge.

The Invader was on Kernowland's sovereign soil.

The Guerreros and their battlebulls headed for Bodmin Moor.

FORTY-TWO

The Guillotine Of Sirap

'Well, Your Majesticness,' began Scurvy, as two trickles of blood dripped down his chin, 'I'm very sorry to report that young Prince Louis stole the spare key when we first encountered him.'

'That blasted boy again,' complained Manaccan. 'That would explain how he vanished into thin air.'

'Yes, he's a spellcaster!' blurted Mrs Maggitt.

'Quiet woman,' shushed her husband.

'No, no,' continued Manaccan, with a dismissive wave of his hand. 'What I mean is that he very likely used the key to escape down into the Golden Cavern. And if he's gone through the Crystal Door, he could be anywhere in Erthwurld by now.'

'Perhaps, your Majesticness,' proposed Lister, 'we could offer a wurldwide reward for him, dead or alive. Then we'll soon have him back here; or his head at any rate.'

'Yes, and the Guillotine of Sirap is on its way, sire,' grovelled Scurvy, as a third trickle of blood ran down his chin from the side of his mouth. 'If his head is still on his shoulders, perhaps one of my first duties as Chief of Police could be to CHOP IT OFF!'

'Splendid thinking, Scurvy,' commended Manaccan. 'You're going to do very well in the new Kernowland. I'll make it a public execution to show what will happen to anyone who gets in my way.'

Scurvy straightened his back and basked in his leader's praise. The other traitors murmured approval and nodded to show they thought that chopping off Louis' head was a very good idea indeed.

FORTY-THREE

The Great Wall of Kernow

Every four hundred paces along the Great Wall of Kernow, there was a Tamar Turret. Private Will Withiel had raised the alarm by ringing his turret bell as soon as he had seen the enemy march over the horizon.

'INVADERS!

'CANNON ON THE HILLS!'

The turrets were hurriedly manned by other members of the Border Battalion. Kernowland's cannon were moved into battle position at intervals along the wall. Within minutes of the alarm, the Kernbowmen, musketeers, and other brave soldiers of the Border Battalion, stood ready.

BOOOOOOMMMMM!

Bombardum was fired first.

WHHZZZZZZZZZZZZZZZZZZ!

A huge ball of iron shot through the air towards the thick wooden door at Launceston Gate.

Boom! Boom! Boom! Boom! Boom! Boom!

The Carnage Cannon were fired immediately after Bombardum.

Whzzz! Whzzz! Whzzz! Whzzz! Whzzz! Whzzz!

Sixty-six balls of iron screamed through the air towards the turrets of the Great Wall of Kernow.

Boom! Boom! Boom! Boom! Boom! Boom!

Swoosh! Swoosh! Swoosh! Swoosh! Swoosh! Swoosh!

The cannon and giant catapults of Kernowland replied.

Along the southern part of the Great Wall, the lookouts had also seen the invaders on the hills.

Captain Crantock of the Tamar Territorials surveyed the enemy horde through his extendable eye-glass.

He reported aloud to his sergeant.

'Zulus, perhaps five thousand. And they've brought rhinophants, hyenajackals, polecats, caracals, bat-eared foxes, wild huntingdogs, sabre-toothed baboons, a whole Animal Army. And they have air power... giant bloodguzzling hairybats.'

As Bombardum and the carnage cannon of the Angles began pounding the Great Wall to the north, Generalchief Shakabantu made ready to attack.

Shakabantu liked to lead from the front. From his standing position in the saddlebox of the foremost rhinophant, he raised his longspear and gave the order.

'CHAAAAAAAAAAAARRRRRRRRRRRRGE!'

The ground shook, and mud and dust flew into the air as two hundred and twenty rhinophants began pounding at full speed across the fields towards the Great Wall of Kernow.

'EEEEEEOOOOOOAAAAAAHHHHHH!'

The rhinophants raised their heads and trumpeted.

The Zulus – the infantry running, and the cavalry riding giant zebrorses – followed on behind. Charging alongside and amongst the Zulus towards The Wall, were the ravenous, raging beasts of the Animal Army.

As the charge began, hundreds of bloodguzzling hairybats sprang off the ground and into the air. They followed their leader, Shlurp, flying only a few feet above the stampeding army of Acirfa.

The shields of the Zulu warriors, covered in leopardskin, were held in front of them. They wore leopardskin warcloth and hollered their battlecry as they advanced on the wall.

'ZZUULLUU! ZZUULLUU! ZZUULLUU!'

For the defenders on the Great Wall, the sight and sound of the flapping hairybats, trumpeting rhinophants, and hollering Zulus was truly terrifying.

'EEEEEEOOOOOOOAAAAAAHHHHHH!'

'ZZUULLUU! ZZUULLUU! ZZUULLUU!'

As the huge battering beasts rumbled towards them – followed by the rest of the running and riding Zulus and the charging and flapping Animal Army of Acirfa – the Kernbowmen made ready.

Captain Crantock calmed his archers.

'Steadyyyyyyyyyyyyyyy… Load… Aim…

'ARROWS AWAY!'

On the captain's order, a hailstorm of Kernish arrows flew into the air, arcing through the sky before raining down on the charging invaders. The Kernowbow was a deadly weapon. Hundreds of the enemy were slain by the first arrowstorm.

But The Invader came on relentlessly, in hordes.

Although Kernowland could not have asked more of its brave soldiers, the sheer number of attackers was overwhelming.

So it was that, despite the brave and fierce resistance of the defenders on the Great Wall, the Angles and Zulus and the Animal Army eventually fought their way across the river, broke down Launceston Gate, and overran the Tamar Turrets.

The Border Battalion was massacred without mercy.

With the contest for The Wall over, the hungry beasts of the Animal Army were free to gorge themselves on the flesh of the Kernowfolk in the border towns… one adult or two children each as they had been promised.

FORTY-FOUR

Titles For Traitors

Pemberley was still peeping.

Drym put his hand up as if he were in class trying to get the teacher's attention.

'Yes, Drym,' said Manaccan.

'Your Majesticness, you were kind enough to say we would all be well rewarded for helping, oh yes you did. Well sire, I was just wondering if you could confirm our new positions and titles?'

A faint smirk came over Manaccan's face. He knew he could get this lot to do what he wanted by appealing to their nasty natures.

'Yes I can, Drym. Only fair, I suppose. Let's go along the line, shall we?

'Mr and Mrs Maggitt, I hereby appoint you *Maggitt & Maggitt, Slave Auctioneers*, just as you requested.

'Mr Scurvy, you are, from this point on, *Superintendent Scurvy, Chief of Police.*'

As the King went along the line, Drym could hardly contain himself. It would soon be his turn. Wealth. Power. Position. Thousands of Kernowkids passing through his dripping dungeon on their way to slavery around the wurld. All his dreams were coming true!

The nasty dustman was rapidly brought back from his thoughts as Manaccan spoke again.

'Dr Lizard will be *Chief Scientist and Mutationeer* at Goonhilly.'

Lizard grinned and looked around at everyone, as if he thought they should all be as pleased for him as he was for himself.

Meanwhile, Manaccan continued.

'Wizard Violothan is henceforth the *King's Chief Wizard and Protector* – Dark Wizard, of course, but no one will know that apart from us to start with.'

At that very moment, a little grey mouse – which had ventured from the safety of its hole looking for food – scurried along in front of the throne. Violothan immediately gripped the heavy black stone in his pocket, drew his wand, pointed, and yelled at the top of his voice: 'Death by Skotos, *die mouse!*'

The Dark Beam lasered towards the mouse and it was instantly frizzled.

'I hate mice!' said Manaccan meanly, as he booted the tiny corpse away from him. The dead mouse slid along the floor and down the steps in front of the throne as Manaccan continued to confirm titles for the traitors. 'Now, let me see, who was next?

'Oh yes, of course, Miss Wendron. You will be *Regulator of Schools*, with a salary and pension package to match the importance of the position.'

'And could I just ask…' began Wendron.

'No need, no need,' interrupted Manaccan, as if he knew exactly what the wrinkled witch was going to say. 'Lister has your Sky Safety Certificate in hand. Henceforth and forthwith, Skycycles will be certified as airworthy and you will be free to sell them anywhere and everywhere.'

Wendron smirked: 'Thank you, your Majesticness, thank you.'

As Wendron and the King conversed, Drym actually found himself, if he were honest, feeling a bit sorry for the children of Kernowland who would now have to go to schools run by Miss

Wendron. Having been her long-suffering pupil when he was young, he didn't envy the children at all. But he didn't dwell on that thought for very long, because he was by now almost beside himself with glee in anticipation of his own title being confirmed.

'Squire Warleggan, I hereby appoint you *General Warleggan*... and, as promised, you will be the highest ranking officer in Kernowland.'

Warleggan grinned his insane grin. At last, he could get his own back on the army that had rejected him; he'd make their lives hell! The warty warlock reached into a pocket and removed a red Evstika armband.

'I admire your enthusiasm, General,' said Manaccan, when he saw the armband, 'but, as you'll no doubt appreciate, we're not quite ready to display our allegiance to the Emperor just yet. However, if all goes to plan, we'll *all* be wearing the mark of Evile by the end of this momentous day.'

Warleggan nodded once to show he understood and quickly pocketed the armband with a slightly embarrassed look on his warty face.

Such treachery! Behind the picture, Pemberley's blood had now reached boiling point as the King continued.

'So, that brings us to Mr Drym. You are hereby appointed *Slaver-in-Chief to the Crown* and granted the first, and exclusive, *Kernowland Slavery Franchise*.'

Drym was ecstatic. He could hardly believe it. The bully had never achieved anything very much before, but now he was going to be a really important person with a title and everything.

'And will I be able to take one child from every family, as promised, Your Majesticness?'

'Yes, yes. Indeed, yes. I know the Emperor wants us to start as he means us to go on in Kernowland. He has decreed in his *Edict Number 1* – Mr Lister has all the Edicts in his attaché case – that one child from every family will be sold into slavery. However, as proof of his kind and considerate nature, he will allow the parents to *choose* which of their children is sold.'

'Oh, that's very fair, very fair,' agreed the traitors as they all nodded to each other at the same time.

'Now, to something important,' said the King. 'Half of everything you make will be for the Royal Tax Coffers, as discussed previously. Agreed?'

'Mmmm,' murmured the line in apparent acquiescence.

Secretly, however, although none dared express it openly, most of the other traitors thought that the King's tax share was a bit excessive. On the other hand, they all knew that they were getting good titles and salaries and – even with so much tax to pay on their normal earnings – they could make an awful lot of money from undisclosed bribes and corruption in their new positions. So perhaps the prospects weren't so bad.

'And just to make sure we add everything up properly,' warned Manaccan, as if he knew what the other traitors were thinking about his share, 'Mr Lister will be continuing in his role as the *King's Counterupper*. But he'll now be working for a different King of course; namely, ME!

'And that brings me to me. Henceforth, I shall be known as *Manaccan the Merciless*. The very name should let people know what will happen if they don't do what they're told.'

'Oh, they will, your Merciless Majesticness, oh yes they will,' fawned Drym. 'And may I just say how grateful I am to you for giving me this opportunity to help with your plans, oh yes I am.'

All in the line quickly mumbled a similar expression of their appreciation. They didn't want to let Drym get away with doing all the toadying.

'Well, as I always like to say,' preened Manaccan, soaking up the grovelling gratitude of the other traitors, 'you scratch my back, and I'll scratch mine.'

There was an awkward silence as the other traitors wondered if they had heard Manaccan the Merciless correctly. Of course, no one dared mention that they thought the King may have got his saying slightly wrong, so nothing was said for quite a few moments.

In the silence, the King looked down on the group of conspirators before him with disdain and derision. Anyone who knew his private plans would have known that the arch schemer had meant exactly what he said.

* * *

Pemberley made his way down the secret corridor, all the while trying to decide whom he could trust and what best to do about the treachery unfolding in the Throne Room.

FORTY-FIVE

A Clever Plan

Clevercloggs and Misty were hiding in Mr Bude's shed, waiting for the return of the old gardener, who had gone to find someone they all knew would be loyal to Kernowland under any circumstances.

'Ah, Pemberley, just the man we need,' greeted Clevercloggs, as the tall butler entered, shortly followed by Mr Bude.

Clevercloggs explained all that had happened and everything he knew from the diary.

Pemberley reciprocated, telling in great detail what he had seen through his peephole. He finished his story with: '*And* I'm afraid Manaccan's protector is Violothan. *And* he's really a Dark Wizard. *And* he has Skotos, the Death Stone.'

'And what news of Princess Kea?' asked Clevercloggs.

'They've put her in the same dungeon as Mr Sand. I'm sure she'll be tending to his wounds, but I overheard the guards speaking and they don't expect him to live beyond this night unless he gets proper medical treatment. But King Manaccan has refused it.'

'I see,' said Clevercloggs. 'Well, we know that the traitors have been making plans. However, I now have a plan of my own. And we have two major advantages over these ten treacherous traitors... they don't know we know, and they don't know we're here.'

With that, the wise old gnome quickly explained his clever plan.

FORTY-SIX

Dodging Donkeys

Colonel Crackington of the 21st Donkeyteers had received a pigeon informing him that the infamous Guerreros and their battlebulls were heading for Bodmin Moor.

He had not yet heard that the Great Wall had fallen.

The colonel and his cavalry rode like the wind to engage the enemy on the moor.

They had found a suitable place for a battle, taken the low ground at the bottom of a steep hill, and were waiting in a long line.

A little while later, The Invader came into view on the brow of the hill, and halted. It was an awesome sight… one thousand battlebulls, each with a Guerrero lancer sitting on its bare back, stretched along the horizon.

On the hill, El Toro's warriors gripped the reins of their battlebulls tightly, holding their lances vertically as they readied themselves for the battle to come.

These fearsome fighters were known around the wurld as 'The Grizzly Guerreros' – or, more often, simply, 'The Grizzlies' – because of their pitiless ferocity during and after battles.

SNORT!

One thousand battlebulls snorted in unison.

STOMP!

One thousand battlebulls stomped in unison.

Seeing the Grizzlies on top of the hill facing them, and hearing the terrifying snorting and stomping of the battlebulls, all the donkeyteers were understandably very afraid.

But they were soon made to forget their fear by the command of their senior officer.

'Red flags… RAISE!' bellowed Colonel Crackington.

At the command, all the donkeyteers raised red flags which were draped along thin poles that they held out to the side with their left hands. Then they all waved the flags so they fluttered provocatively in the breeze, before lowering the poles to their sides again.

'They taunt us and mock us, my General,' mumbled Gordo, to his leader through a mouthful of food, as he glared down the hill at the mounted Land Guardians of Kernow.

'NO PRISONERS!' bawled El Toro, as loud as he could.

'ATAQUE!'

With that, one thousand battlebulls charged down the hill at the donkeyteers.

'Stand steady, men of Kernow,' calmed the Colonel at the bottom of the hill.

'Stand steadyyy.'

Even though their training had taught them what to do, this was *real* war, and the bulls were now getting far too close for comfort for some of the donkeyteers. But they bravely held the line.

'Steadyyyyyyyyy!'

The donkeyteers continued to hold the line.

'DODGE!'

On the Colonel's signal, as the battlebulls reached them, all the donkeys suddenly dodged to the right and the donkeyteers raised the red flags on their poles to the left again.

The battlebulls seemed totally confused by this dodging

manoeuvre and they all ran straight at the red flags. But there was nothing behind the flags when the charging bulls arrived and, as each made contact with the cloth, the donkeyteers let go of the poles and stuck their swords into the necks of the mutant bovine beasts as hard as they could.

Over two hundred battlebulls fell in this first charge.

Those Guerreros who had not fallen, regrouped, and a brutal battle began.

After much fierce fighting, the donkeyteers – all darting about on their little dodging donkeys – actually began to get the better of the supposedly 'invincible' Guerreros on their enormous battlebulls.

Then, just as the donkeyteers were near to celebrating a famous victory, Colonel Crackington saw four dozen ramdragons flying over the hills from the north.

And, straight ahead, over the hills from the east, fresh from their success at the Great Wall of Kernow, flew a hundred or more giant bloodguzzling hairybats, all flapping their wings rapidly as they followed Shlurp into the fray.

'Enemy in the sky,' shouted the colonel.

FORTY-SEVEN

Destination Dungeons

Misty knew the castle like the back of his paw. He carried a note addressed to Princess Kea in his mouth as he scampered along corridors and under doors en route to his destination… the dungeons.

The brave blue mouse arrived in the dungeons without incident.

But, unfortunately, as he got to the door, the guard spotted him, jumped off his chair, and tried to stomp on the scurrying mouse with his big boot. Luckily, the portly guard made so much noise getting off his chair before he raised his foot – and was so slow in stomping it down – that Misty was able to dodge the stomp and dive under the door. The guard was in two minds whether to open the door to get the mouse. Luckily for Misty, he had nothing in particular against mice, and decided against it.

In the dungeon corridor, Misty quickly found the cell which imprisoned Princess Kea and Mr Sand.

He saw the princess tenderly tending to Mr Sand's knife wound. The Chief Surveyor and Mapmaker was lying face down on a bed of straw. The princess was so involved in what she was doing that Misty initially had trouble getting her attention… so, in the end, he resorted to scampering right over her foot!

'Eeeeeek!'

That did the trick. She shrieked as she jumped back in surprise and shock; but quickly regained her composure when she saw it was only a little blue mouse.

Misty dropped the note on the floor at the princess' feet. She picked it up and read its contents.

I'm Misty. I've been sent by Clevercloggs. There are loyal Kernowfolk in the castle. We have a plan...

After Princess Kea had read the rest of the note explaining the plan, she bent down and put the back of her hand on the floor so that Misty could scamper on to her palm.

Then the princess raised Misty up in her hand and brought him close to her nose. A blue haze was already forming around Misty as he prepared himself to help Mr Sand. Princess Kea had heard about the healing power of blue mice but had never seen one in action.

As she placed him gently on Mr Sand's back, Misty ran straight to the wound that would soon drain the life from the kindly old man.

The princess watched in awe as – after a few twitches of Misty's whiskers – the wound began to heal itself, as if by magic.

A few moments later, Mr Sand groaned as he started to regain consciousness.

'Orrrgghhhh.'

FORTY-EIGHT

Snoring Pie

Pemberley was carrying the cleverpotion that Clevercloggs had mixed together from a number of bottles of liquid he had in his rucksack. The brave butler was on his way to see Mrs Portwrinkle. Everyone had unanimously agreed that the jolly old cook would be loyal to Kernowland and would help with the clever plan.

In the kitchen, Mrs Portwrinkle's loyalty was confirmed as soon as Pemberley told her the story. She readily agreed to put the Snoring Potion in a pie for the dungeon guard. Armed with the pie on a platter, Pemberley set out for the dungeon.

Meanwhile, Clevercloggs had gone down into the sewers. Mr Bude had pointed out a sewer entrance only a few paces from the shed, and the gnome had been able to get to it without being seen. He was now under the iron drainage grate – in the centre of the dungeon corridor – that was used by the guards when sloshing out the cells. The clever gnome was waiting patiently for the snoring to start.

'With the compliments of Mrs Portwrinkle for dutiful guards,' said Pemberley, as he put the steaming pie right under the hungry man's nose.

'Splendid!' said the guard. 'Please pass on my thanks to Mrs Portwrinkle.'

'Certainly,' said Pemberley, who then left and walked back up the steps into the castle.

The aroma of the pie was wonderful, and the guard couldn't

resist tasting it without delay. Almost instantly, after just one bite of the pastry, he was asleep in his chair and snoring loudly.

As soon as he heard the snoring, Clevercloggs went into action. Although the old gnome had bad legs, he was blessed with incredibly strong arms – even at his age, he could still bench press four times his own weight – which he used to pull himself up the iron laddersteps and through the sewer grate. Hobbling on his sticks, he then made his way to the cell containing Misty, Mr Sand, and Princess Kea.

'Hurry, Misty,' he whispered when he got to the cell.

Misty knew exactly what he had to do. The little mouse scampered across the big cobbles of the cell, out through the bars and along the corridor to the locked door between him and the snoring guard. He squeezed under the door, climbed up the guard's leg and grabbed the dungeon keys in his jaws. The keys were on a big key ring and were very heavy. As he dragged them towards the guard's knee, the weight was too much for him and he plummeted, with the keys still in his mouth, to the floor.

Luckily the brave blue mouse wasn't hurt and he had just enough strength left to drag the keys under the door, where Clevercloggs was now waiting as planned.

Clevercloggs took the keys and released Princess Kea and Mr Sand from the cell.

'Am I glad to see you, Clevercloggs,' said Mr Sand in a croaky voice.

'Likewise,' agreed Princess Kea.

'No time to talk at the moment, I'm afraid,' said Clevercloggs. With that, he locked the cell door and hobbled back to the wooden dungeon door at the end of the corridor, where Misty was waiting.

Clevercloggs put the keys in the little mouse's mouth and Misty dragged them under the door and deposited them by the boot of the still snoring guard. Then he ran back under the door where Clevercloggs picked him up and pocketed him as he said with a chuckle:

'I'd bet my beard the guard will think he just dropped the door keys while he was asleep; so it will seem as if the prisoners have just disappeared into thin air!'

Back at the cell, Clevercloggs gave instructions.

'Quickly Your Highness, Gwithian, down through the grate.'

Princess Kea went first, waiting at the bottom on the iron rungs of the laddersteps to help Mr Sand in case he fell.

Clevercloggs followed, with Misty and the Golden Key safely in his pocket.

As they made their way through the sewers, the old gnome explained more about his plan for their escape from the castle.

They all agreed that, taking into account everything they knew, there was only one place in Erthwurld they should try to get to.

When they got back to the laddersteps below the sewer entrance near the shed, Clevercloggs reached for a big bag that he had left tied to one of the iron rungs and took out some clothes.

'Here, change into these.'

FORTY-NINE

The Battle of Bodmin Moor

The roaring ramdragons and swarming hairybats joined the fight against Crackington's plucky donkeyteers with savage ferocity.

The ramdragons breathed fire as they tore donkeyteers from their saddles with their long sharp talons and butted them with their horns.

The hairybats, with hookclaws extended, landed on the backs of the cavalrymen, and sank long sharp vampire fangs deep into the flesh of their necks, before sucking every last drop of blood from their bodies.

To the donkeyteers, it seemed like their attackers were everywhere at once. In the face of such crushing odds, the courageous men of Kernow didn't stand a chance.

Then, as if from nowhere, choughateers arrived in the sky and joined the battle. Furious dog-fights began in the skies above the moor.

Ter-ter-terrrrr!

Ter-ter-terrrrr!

A Kernish Infantry bugle sounded an attack, and the donkeyteers heard the welcome sound of the Kernowdrum beating out the march of the Land Guardians as General Gorran-Haven now led a huge contingent of Kernish land forces over a hill to join the battle.

Kernbowmen brought hairybats crashing to the ground.

Kernish artillery guns aimed shots at the lower flying

ramdragons and Gorran-Haven's musketeers picked off Guerreros, who fell dead and dying from the backs of their steeds.

The body count grew as the battle raged on.

All the while, the silent vulturerats circled above the battlefield, waiting patiently, ominously, for the fighting to end.

With the arrival of the Land Guardian reinforcements, the Kernish forces began to gain the upper hand.

But their success was destined to be short-lived.

For now, over the hills from the east, came the massed forces of the Angles and the Zulus and the Animal Army.

Following their victory at the Great Wall, Generals Angar and Shakabantu had made their way as fast as possible to join the Battle of Bodmin Moor.

The arrival of the massed forces of The Invader from the east proved decisive. And so it was that, after hours of fierce fighting, as the sun set over Kernowland on Darkness Day, the brave defenders were finally defeated.

As was always the way with the Grizzly Guerreros, no prisoners were taken and none of the wounded was allowed to live. Not a soldier nor a donkey, not an airman nor a chough, survived.

The Guardians of Kernow had fought with incredible courage in defence of the land they loved… and *all* had paid the ultimate price.

After the battle, as the victors moved on towards Kernow Castle and the capital city, Truro, the circling vulturerats finally descended and landed on Kernowland's soil… to begin their gruesome work.

FIFTY

Outlaws in Disguise

Mr Bude was performing his part in the clever plan.

He made his way around to the back of the armoury, picked the lock of the door and entered. Here, he gathered up weapons and put them carefully under the garden implements in his wheelbarrow.

Then he covered the wheelbarrow with a sack – so that just the spade, fork, and hoe handles were sticking out from beneath it – and made his way back to his shed.

It was slightly nerve-wracking, even for a brave old soldier such as Bartholomew Bude, to move about the castle with stolen weapons in his wheelbarrow. But it seemed that nobody was giving a second thought to the familiar old gardener going about his business.

Old Bart arrived back at his shed, emptied his wheelbarrow, and began hiding the weapons in a cupboard.

There was a knock at the door.

Bude hid the weapons quickly and answered the door.

There before him was a mother in a shawl, carrying an infant wrapped in a big cloth. The woman was accompanied by an old monk with a long staff.

Mr Bude smiled: 'Very convincing.'

* * *

'Ha-ha-ha!' Inside the shed, the gardener laughed heartily.

The mother had dropped the shawl from her head. It was Princess Kea in a wig. In her arms, she was carrying Clevercloggs, who was pretending to be her child. And the old monk with the staff was really Mr Sand!

'Quickly, speed is of the essence, before they realise the prisoners have escaped,' chivvied Clevercloggs. 'From your reaction, Bart, these disguises seem to be believable. Now we just have to get past the guards and into the castle. Remember, they've been told that all three of us are murderers. They won't hesitate to kill us on sight. Do you all remember what to say if we are challenged?'

Everyone confirmed they knew what to say as Princess Kea and Mr Sand armed themselves with some of the weapons collected by Mr Bude.

'You'll need all the weapons you can carry in the hunting grounds of Erthwurld,' advised the old soldier. 'I've seen a chewing creature or two in my time.'

Clevercloggs, however, declined to take even a short dagger.

'I have my own cleverweapons in my rucksack,' he said. 'They've protected me for hundreds of years, so I should think they'll be up to the task on this little adventure.'

Princess Kea and Mr Sand smiled knowingly at each other, both suddenly remembering that they were in the presence of a living legend... *Clevercloggs the Explorer!*

A few minutes later, the outlaws in disguise left the shed and made their way towards the entrance to the Dome Tower.

FIFTY-ONE

Escape to Jungleland

There was a lot of noise and confusion in the castle as the evening drew in. What with the explosion in the Prism Chamber earlier in the day, the dark cloud floating ominously above the Dome Tower, the death of the King, invasion warnings, talk of three dangerous traitors in the dungeons, and one murderous young killer on the loose, the castle inhabitants had plenty to think about.

A story had circulated that the defenders on The Great Wall, the coasts, and Bodmin Moor had already lost the battles to defend Kernowland.

The order from the new King was then confirmed in a proclamation: 'Further resistance is futile. Make preparations to welcome Emperor Evile's forces when they arrive, so that peace negotiations can be undertaken.'

The courageous Guardians at the castle, especially Lieutenant Liskeard, were not at all happy with this order. However, the new King was in charge, and they were trained to obey their leaders, so all the soldiers reluctantly did as instructed.

Soon everyone was scurrying about, readying the castle with welcoming banners and preparing for a Banquet of Peace.

Just as Clevercloggs had planned, the bustling upheaval in the courtyard allowed the outlaws in disguise to reach the grand arch at the entrance to the Corridor of the Ancestors unchallenged and without other incident.

The two guards at the grand arch were not overly suspicious.

They were, after all, looking out for Prince Louis, the dangerous killer, not an old monk and a woman with a sick child.

Nevertheless, the guards had to do their duty, and the corporal challenged the mother before him.

'Identify yourselves and state your business in the castle.'

'My son is sick. He needs to see Dr Looe.'

'What's wrong with him?' asked the corporal, making as if to pull back the cloth and look at the face of the child.

'Purplepox!' murmured Mr Sand, in an intentionally croaky voice.

'PURPLEPOX!' exclaimed both guards at once, as they took several steps backwards.

'Yes, the purple boils began this morning,' added Princess Kea. 'It's taken us most of the day to get here. So you see it's very important that the doctor sees him straight away; we don't have much time.'

The guards looked at each other with dread; quite understandably, neither wanted to catch purplepox. It was a horrible way to die. The boils spread quickly all over your body, itching and burning terribly as they released their poison into your blood. If not treated with 'Purplepox Powder' within a day, the condition was normally fatal. And, even if the medicine were administered in time, the chances were still only fifty-fifty.

'Very well, you may pass. Quickly, get him to the doctor. Go on madam. Quickly!'

Having got past the guards, the three outlaws made their way briskly along the Corridor of the Ancestors.

'I can't carry you much further,' gasped Princess Kea to the bundle in her arms.

'Not far now,' replied the bundle.

When they reached the doors into the Welcome Hall, Mr Sand opened them a crack and peered through to see if Pemberley had made the rendezvous on time.

As planned, the tall butler soon entered through the main archway and strode across the hall towards the doors. He pushed one of the doors and put his head around it into the corridor.

'Make haste, if you please.'

With that, Pemberley led the three outlaws through one of the twelve doors that lined the walls of the Welcome Hall.

A few paces down another corridor, the butler pulled a candle holder protruding from the wall. A secret doorway opened in the wall, which led to a secret passageway.

'In here, quickly please.'

They all entered the passageway.

'Ohhhh, at last!' exclaimed Princess Kea, as she set Clevercloggs down on the floor.

'Heavy little bundle, aren't I?' said the old gnome.

'I'll say,' replied the princess.

'Solid muscle, that's what makes me so heavy!' quipped Clevercloggs, with a self-deprecating smile.

Pemberley led the way up some steps, and then they had to climb a rope ladder through a hole between the floors to another passageway.

At the end of that passageway was another secret door.

'I should go first,' said Pemberley, 'to make sure the coast is clear.'

The butler opened the door into the Map Room, quickly closing it behind him in case there was anyone there. But the room was empty and he opened the door again to let the others enter.

'You should leave us now, Pemberley,' advised Clevercloggs.

'Wouldn't do to arouse suspicions; you're much more useful to our cause in your normal job here than in a dungeon.'

'Understood,' agreed the brave and loyal butler.

'We'll done, Pemberley, excellent show,' praised the Princess.

'Thank you, your Highness, and good luck to you all on your journey.'

With that, Pemberley left the room via the secret doorway.

Clevercloggs used the Golden Key to open the locktile and they all proceeded down through the trapdoor in the Mosaic Map. They hurried along the passageway and descended the stone stairway into the Golden Cavern.

The three outlaws all linked arms as they approached the Crystal Door along the golden paving slabs.

'We can only hope that both Tizzie and Louis are on their way to Jungleland,' said Clevercloggs, as Misty peered inquisitively out over the brim of his pocket.

'And we must try to find Jack Truro, the Red Wizard's Apprentice,' added Mr Sand. 'He's the last of the Rainbow Wizards and, although he probably doesn't know it yet, the last hope for Kernowland and the wurld.'

'Nwotegroeg, Aibmag, Jungleland, Acirfa,' said Clevercloggs.

As it softened, the courageous heroes stepped into the Crystal Door.

FIFTY-TWO

Tunnel Rock

As *The Revenger* sailed further south, the heat on board became more and more stifling. Although she knew that hers was the next-but-one name on the rota, Tizzie was glad it wasn't yet her turn to clean the hold and empty the stinking buckets. She wasn't at all sure she'd be able to face it without being sick.

On deck once more, Tizzie could see they were approaching a heavily fortified peninsula. Jack explained to the group: 'That's the Rock of Ratlarbig; which means we're already off the south coast of Niaps. Juan, you're from there, can you give a lesson for the younger ones?'

Juan came to the front and began talking.

'Gather round, those who need to learn.'

About twenty of the younger children formed a tightly packed circle around Juan. The older children half-listened from where they were, since they knew most of what he was teaching. Tizzie stayed outside of the circle, so as not to arouse suspicion, but made sure she got close enough to hear everything.

'As you all know,' explained Juan, 'we're heading for Jungleland, which is on the continent of Acirfa; but it looks like we'll be stopping off at Ratlarbig. This is a strategically important fortified peninsula, because it guards the entrance to the Naenarretidem Sea, which separates the continents of Eporue and Acirfa. Although the rock is only two kiloms long, and one wide, below it are kilom upon kilom of criss-cross tunnels at various depths. That's why it is better known around the wurld as "Tunnel Rock". The tunnels are supposed to be Top Secret, but it's the worst kept secret in the world. Everybody knows about them. Most people don't know what's actually in the tunnels, but many believe that Evile stores special weapons there, left over from the Science Wars. Some say he's been developing a new breed of Chewing Creature in the deepest tunnels... for the colosseums.'

'Chewing Creatures,' trembled one of the younger children, as if the very mention of the mutant beasts was enough to scare her out of her skin, 'I don't want to stop there.'

'Well, I'm afraid we're going to have to because Pigleg wants to collect something,' said Jack to the class, speaking in a low voice. 'It's a new type of gun called a "Thunder Blunderbuss". They say it's powerful enough to fell a chewing creature at fifty paces... if you're brave enough to get that close.'

'Si,' confirmed Juan, 'Jenny said it makes a sound like thunder.'

'Pigleg's already given the gun a name... *Blunder Bess*,' continued Jack. 'Tells everyone he called her that because she's noisy and dangerous... just like his girlfriend, Big Bessie.'

Tizzie had never imagined Pigleg would have a girlfriend! She listened intently as Juan spoke again.

'Blunder Bess could be big enough to finish Big Red Grunter off. Trouble is, she sprays marble-sized, lead shotballs all over the place. If any of us is tied up as bait when he pulls the trigger, we'll likely as not be in the firing line. Any one of those shotballs could kill us if we're hit. Pigleg won't care though, he'll be more concerned with making sure he gets Grunter.'

'So that's why we need to have a plan,' advised Jack. 'We've been trying to think of one. If any of you younger kids thinks up a good plan, make sure you share it straight away.'

Tizzie couldn't help wondering what would be worse: being eaten bit by bit by Big Red Grunter or killed by a stray shotball from Blunder Bess. The gun would at least be quicker. Unless she were wounded? She now began to worry about that too, as Juan shared some more information with the group.

'Pigleg can't set foot on Ratlarbig. When he was here last, he had a fight with an Imperial Navy captain who was making eyes at Big Bessie. Pigleg's very jealous. They say he nearly stomped the man to death with his hoof.'

As if to confirm Juan's statement, *The Revenger* didn't make for port as it approached Ratlarbig. Instead, the pirate vessel sailed to a quiet inlet and weighed anchor.

Two men were sent ashore in a rowing boat. They returned within the hour. A box was hauled on board. It had a picture of what Tizzie presumed was a blunderbuss painted down both sides.

'Arrh! There's me blazin' beauty!' exclaimed Captain Pigleg as he opened the lid and inspected the contents of the box. 'That pig'll be pork in no time when I introduce 'im to *Blunder Bess*.'

With the new weapon securely stowed aboard, Tugger and Trailblazer pulled *The Revenger* out of the inlet, and the pirate ship set sail for the open seas once more.

'Look! Over there,' whispered Juan to the younger children as the slaves were ordered to get below, 'that's the coast of Acirfa. Won't be long now until we're in Jungleland.'

'Yes, but Jenny's just told me we'll be stopping off for two days at Acnalbasac City in Sandland on the way,' added Jack.

'Why?' asked little Lucy.

Tizzie was greatly concerned by her friend's reply.

'Slave school.'

FIFTY-THREE

Port of Acnalbasac

As *The Revenger* sailed in to the Port of Acnalbasac, more lessons were taking place in the hold. Mustafa, a Brownskin of about fourteen, was teaching the younger children.

'Acnalbasac is the largest city in the country of Occorom. It lies on the western coast of the Sandland Sector, on the continent of Acirfa.

'The city's economy is based on two things. The main one, as you'll all probably know, is slavery; the people of Sandland are the best slave traders and trainers in the wurld. Can anybody tell me what the second major industry in Occorom is?'

'Mining?' chirped Matsaru Kawasaki, a boy from the Napaj Islands.

'Quite right, Mat,' said Mustafa. 'The phosphate mines are terrible places where the slave-miners have to dig out the phosphate rock for sixteen hours a day. The life expectancy of a slave-miner is less than two years. Does anybody know what phosphate is used for?'

Yang put his hand up.

'To make fertiliser for the Emperor's factory farms.'

'That's right, very good,' confirmed Mustafa, as he continued the lesson. 'The main market is in the centre of the city. It's officially called the "Anfa Souk", but it's better known around the world as the "Bizarre Bazaar", because of all the strange things on sale.

'The bazaar is an infamous place. They say you can buy anything there, for the right price. Of course the price depends on how well you can haggle and barter. I should think Pigleg will be stocking up on supplies of all sorts of things; he loves haggling and bartering.'

Through the open hatch, they now heard Captain Pigleg's booming voice: 'Get them slaves yoked and ready for disembarkin'!'

Mr Cudgel passed the Captain's order on.

'Purgy, you heard the Cap'n. It's time for the neck irons. They're going to slave school.'

The tattooed enforcer came down into the hold with two other pirates. The trio went to a chest and took out a number of old and rusty iron neck braces, and a long thick chain. The chain had a padlock at each end.

The pirates put the iron bands around the necks of the children, who were then made to stand one pace apart in order of height, shortest at the front, tallest at the back.

Purgy threaded the chain between small rings that had been welded to the outer rims of the neck braces. Then he attached each of the two padlocks to the neck brace of the child at either end of the line, locking them securely with the rusty key.

The chain now joined all the children together at the neck.

'Get up on deck… and look lively!' shouted Purgy.

On deck, the frightened children formed a long line, again a pace apart.

'Arrrrr, a slave-chain in neck irons,' sighed Pigleg. 'Warms me heart every time I see one.'

'Quite so, Cap'n,' agreed Mr Cudgel, as he tapped his truncheon arm on his palm.

As the pirates got ready to disembark, they drew lots.

'Jenny said that four of them have to stay behind to guard the ship,' informed Jack. 'None of them wants to stay aboard; they'd much rather go into town.'

As if to prove Jack's point, the four pirates who had drawn the shortest straws seemed very disappointed; Tizzie thought that one of them had tears in his eyes.

Looking around, she also saw that Gurt was wide awake, standing with his arms folded… and Lasher coiled in his hand.

'Move 'em out,' Mr Cudgel.

'Aye, aye Cap'n. Gurt! Get 'em movin'.'

Thwcrack!

With that, the captain's punisher cracked Lasher once. Tizzie thought this must be the signal to start walking because the slave-chain began to shuffle forward. She was in front of Jack.

'Why are we going to slave school?' she whispered, hoping it wasn't something she was supposed to know.

'Some of us will probably survive being boar bait. Pigleg will get a much better price for us if we've got a Slaveworker Certificate and a Slavemark Stamp from the Sandland Slave School. They're going to decide what type of slave jobs we'd each be best suited to, then they'll teach us how to be good at the jobs. The slave school is owned and run by Mafi Mook, who calls himself, "headmaster". He's very nasty and bad tempered, and more than a little "touched" by the sun.

'That's why they call him, "Mad Mafi".'

FIFTY–FOUR

The Bizarre Bazaar

The slave chain of weary children shuffled down the gangplank. With the smallest at the front and the tallest at the back, Tizzie was roughly in the middle. The slave troop was forced to march ahead, with Gurt cracking his whip every twenty paces.

Within the first few minutes, Tizzie counted six other slave chains going towards the port. Some wore neck irons; others were shackled together at the ankles.

The rough and rusty edges of the neck iron had already started to rub Tizzie's skin. It became more raw and sore with every step. The sun bore down on her, burning any exposed flesh not covered by her ragged clothes.

They came to the Anfa Souk. Tizzie tried to take in all the sights, smells, and sounds of the bizarre bazaar. Market stalls covered every inch of ground. The people wore kaftanrobes, djellabarobes, and turbans of all different kinds and colours. A snake charmer played a long, thin flute. There were all sorts of beggars, some sitting, some lying, and some walking around with their begging bowls held out.

A blind man played a stringed instrument as he sat with his begging cup in front of him. Tizzie watched in silent disgust as Purgy took a furtive glance from side to side before quickly crouching to steal some coins from the cup.

'Look, a quadcamel,' said Polly, pointing at a very long camel with four humps being led by a tall man with a brown turban.

'And ponydogs for sale over there!' exclaimed Yang, making it abundantly clear to all that he wanted one.

At a café on the perimeter, lots of men sat outside with small coffee cups in front of them as they read their newspapers. A few played chess or draughts. Some appeared to be smoking something through long tubes connected to large ornate pots.

All around there were huge baskets made of rope topped with rope lids. Carpets, rugs, and mats, some rolled, some flat, were everywhere. The aroma of kebabs wafted from charcoal grates, reminding Tizzie how hungry she was. A vendor was shouting to passers-by: 'Figs, lovely figs. Get your lovely figs here.'

There was a stall selling dates and all types of fruit. Other stalls sold vegetables. Some sold nuts. One displayed sweets, including a huge tower of *Turkish Delight*. Round flatbreads, stacked high on square boards, were balanced expertly on the heads of vendors as they weaved through the throng of people.

At the far end of the bazaar, Pigleg halted his men and the slave chain by raising his golden hook.

'We'll tarry here a while for a peek at the auction. I want to see the going rate for slaves.'

Looking in the same direction as Pigleg, Tizzie saw that, in the far corner of the mud wall that bounded the bazaar, there was a big stage. A banner above the stage read:

HERE TODAY - SLAVE AUCTION

On the stage was a podium. A Whiteskin woman in chains was crying as a chubby young boy of about four was put on the podium. Tizzie thought it must be her son. Up in front of all those people, and with his mother sobbing behind him, it wasn't surprising that the boy started crying too.

'Ten evos for this youngster,' said the auctioneer, as the boy and his mother both sobbed louder and louder.

Tizzie had learned on the ship that a gold coin called an 'evo', with Evile's head on it, was the currency of the Empire. It was worth about the same as a Kernowland crown, the only other currency left in the wurld.

At that price, there were no offers.

'Hand me me pursebag if you'd be so kind, Mr Cudgel,' said Captain Pigleg, a little theatrically, as if he were enjoying a game.

From an inside coat pocket, his first mate withdrew a small leather bag, tied at the top with a draw string.

'Five evos,' offered Pigleg.

'Six,' said someone in the crowd.

'I don't want people forcing the price up unnecessarily,' whispered Pigleg. 'Sort that if you please, gentlemen.'

Cudgel and Purgy walked forward and stood either side of the other bidder, each putting a hand on his shoulder. The man stepped forward and wheeled around, with his curved dagger drawn. But, when he saw Pigleg glaring at him, he quickly replaced his knife in his sash belt and hurried away from the auction.

'Seven,' shouted Pigleg very loudly, as if making sure that everyone knew that it was he, the most notorious pirate in the history of Erthwurld, who wanted the slave boy.

There were no more bids.

'Sold to Captain Pigleg,' said the auctioneer, banging his gavel down hard.

'Sir, have mercy, please,' begged the woman as she ran over

and dropped at the captain's feet. 'Take me too, he's my son; still only a baby. He needs me.'

'Bah, what would I want with her?' said Pigleg, turning his back on the woman and addressing his question to Mr Cudgel as if he couldn't understand why she was even suggesting such a thing. 'She'd be no good for boar bait… far too old.'

Cudgel nodded his head in agreement and pushed the woman away forcefully as she moved forward to plead again.

Pigleg was uncontested as he made bids for six more children.

The new acquisitions were all put in neck irons and slotted into the slave chain in height order.

FIFTY-FIVE

'Mad Mafi' Mook

As the pirates and their slave chain began to move away from the auction area, there was a commotion in the crowd.

The throng parted to allow the passage of a huge round man, who rolled towards them dressed in a green turban, and a long, flowing, pale blue kaftanrobe. On his feet, he wore a pair of dark blue, sequined slippers, which curled up at the toes. A little gold bell was attached to each curl of the slippers. He also had a little gold bell dropping down from the front of his turban, gold bell earrings, and a gold bell bracelet on each wrist. All the gold bells tinkled as he walked.

'There's enough material in that robe to make a tent,' joked Yang. Tizzie and all the other children sniggered.

Thwcrack! Gurt cracked Lasher. The children fell silent.

The rolling gold-bell-man headed straight towards Pigleg.

'Captain! Welcome once again to my humble little city,' he said, as if they were long lost friends meeting at his home, rather than business associates meeting in the main square.

'Greetings, Mook,' roared Pigleg, with equal enthusiasm.

'Can we perhaps do business today, my old friend?' enquired Mafi Mook.

'Possibly,' answered the leader of the pirates. 'It all depends on how many golden evos you have with you today.'

'I am interested in taking a new laundry wife,' declared Mafi, very matter-of-factly. 'My youngest wife, Thinima, is now thirteen.

133

She's moving on from laundry duties to the kitchens. I haven't got very much money to spend, but I like the look of *that* one.'

To her horror, Tizzie realised that the gold-bell-man was pointing at her.

'Arrrrrr, hagglin' and barterin',' said Pigleg with a crooked smile, 'me favourite Sandland game.'

But then his grin faded.

'Now, before we go any further, you know I'm not lettin' go of any bait at any price until I return from Jungleland.'

'Your annual expedition in pursuit of the big pig is well known to me,' said Mafi. 'We can do a deal now and you can deliver the goods on your return. Cash on delivery.'

'Now you're talkin' sense.'

'There is only one condition,' emphasised Mafi Mook, with a very serious look on his own face. 'She must be whole, all four limbs still attached... no good in the laundry without arms and legs, eh my friend?!'

The two men shared an ironic laugh.

'But I mean it,' continued Mad Mafi, switching to a serious tone and staring straight into Pigleg's eyes. 'I won't be paying for damaged goods. You must deliver her back in one piece, exactly as she is now.'

'Agreed... So what's it you're offerin'?'

'Such a scrawny little thing. I will take her off your hands for ten evos.'

The smile drained from Pigleg's face.

'Now, come on, Mook. You'll know full well that I paid more than that for her in the first place. Fifty evos is a fair price for a wife this young. You'll get years of work out of her. Fed and watered her all the way from Kernowland too, remember.'

'True enough… fifteen.'

'Forty.'

'Twenty.'

'Thirty.'

'Done,' said Mafi, licking his right hand and offering it forward.

'Deal,' said Pigleg, doing likewise.

The two men slapped their hands together once, and then shook them vigorously to confirm the bargain.

Tizzie wondered what price Captain Pigleg would have gone down to. Was her life worth only *thirty gold evos* in this horrible place?

For his part, Pigleg seemed somewhat surprised at the speed with which the transaction was completed.

'So, wanted 'er all along, eh?'

'Indeed so,' agreed Mafi, now allowing himself a big, smug smile, as he peered down at Tizzie and pointed and wiggled one of his thick fat fingers at her.

'See you at slave school, laundry wife.'

FIFTY-SIX

The Casablanca Club

Shortly after leaving the bazaar, they passed the *Casablanca Club*. Tizzie could hear strange music coming from inside. There was a poster of a belly dancer on the wall outside, and the pirates all looked at the club longingly. Pigleg seemed sensitive to the wishes of his crew.

'A pirate needs regular rum 'n' belly dancing as much as he needs raidin' 'n' plunderin',' he bellowed. 'Ain't that the truth, men!?'

'Aye, aye, Cap'n,' shouted the men.

Pigleg waved his hook, motioning the pirates towards the door of the club: 'Go on then, in ya go!'

'Thrree cheerrs for the Cap'n.

'Hip, hip, hooree!

'Hip, hip, hooree!

'Hip, hip, hooree!'

Pigleg stuck his chest out and soaked up his men's cheers before speaking again.

'Gurt, you stand guard here, there's a good fellow.'

Gurt nodded, removing Lasher from his belt with his right hand.

Thwcrack! He cracked the whip once, as if to show the children what they could look forward to if they tried to escape.

'Mr Cudgel, get them slaves secured.'

'Purgy, you heard the Cap'n.'

The tattooed pirate produced a rusty old iron key, undid a

padlock and unattached the iron chain from the smallest child, Elsa, who was at the front of the line. He then pushed the little girl towards Gurt, saying: 'Hold that.'

Gurt held on to Elsa by her hair to make sure she didn't run away.

Purgy then fed the chain through an iron ring cemented into the wall of the club, which seemed to have been put there specifically for the purpose. The iron chain was then re-attached to the brace around Elsa's neck with the padlock. The children were now all securely chained to the wall.

The afternoon sun was blazing. The children had had no water for hours. Tizzie's lips were cracking and the skin on her nose was peeling.

With all his fellow crew members inside, and the children chained to the wall, Gurt took the opportunity to get some sleep. He was soon snoring.

'Sleeping as usual,' commented Jack. 'Knows we can't escape when we're chained to the wall.'

'What is this place?' asked Tizzie, nodding her head forwards to make it clear she was asking about the club.

'Well, as you know, Evile normally reverses the names of cities, countries, and continents when he conquers them; to show he's in charge and has total control of absolutely everything, even the names of places. Acnalbasac City was once called "Casablanca". This club was allowed to keep its original name because the owner was a spy for Evile.'

'What's happening inside?' asked Hans, when Jack had finished explaining.

Tizzie was right outside the window, which was set very low in the wall. She peered through the iron bars to see that steps led down from the entrance into a room that was mostly below ground level. Huge fans turned on the ceiling, each powered by a small caged child pulling on a rope. The cages were hanging from the ceiling. She thought it must be a very boring job, being caged up and having to pull on that rope all day, every day.

As Tizzie relayed what she saw to the others, the pirates all began drinking and having a big party. Then the show started. A woman dressed in red silk, with her midriff showing, appeared on the stage. She began to wiggle and wobble her tummy and hips, which Tizzie knew was called a 'belly dance'.

'This is only the warm-up party,' said Jack. 'The real party will begin when we get to the Islands of Airanac. Big Bessy and the other WAGs will all be there waiting.'

'What are WAGs?' asked Tizzie.

'It's short for "wives and girlfriends". Pigleg knows he has to keep his men happy with parties before they go on the hunt for Grunter. The hunt is dangerous for them as well as us. It might be their last chance to see their WAGs.'

'How do you know all this?' asked Tizzie.

'Hans told me. He was one of the first to be captured in the round-up this year. He's been in the hold a long time and learned a lot from overhearing things. Jenny tells me things too, when she gets a chance.'

Jenny, thought Tizzie indignantly, I still don't trust her… and I can't understand why Jack does either.

Tizzie was very tired but, if anything, the noise from the club seemed to be getting louder as time went on.

'Will we be able to sleep soon?'

'Fat chance,' answered Jack, 'they'll be partying in there for most of the night.'

FIFTY-SEVEN

Fort Arahas

It was morning outside the Casablanca Club. Tizzie had been unable to sleep for most of the night. It had been absolutely freezing, and the noise from the club had carried on until the early hours.

Even when the party finally stopped, the scared young girl had lain awake, worrying and worrying again about what might happen to her. To make matters worse, little Elsa had been awake too, constantly crying and asking for her mummy.

Tizzie looked through the bars into the party room. Some pirates were asleep on the tables and floor. Some were sprawled on the stage. Many still clutched clay mugs and empty bottles of drink in their hands.

'Wakey wakey, rise and shine.' Mr Cudgel was now rousing the men by tapping and poking them with his truncheon arm. 'Come on, let's be 'aving yer! Party's over, lads. Form marchin' lines outside.'

Many of the men were finding it hard to wake up.

'NOW! NOW! NOW!'

Bang! Bang! Bang!

As Mr Cudgel shouted, he banged his truncheon arm down on a table three times. This was enough to rouse even the sleepiest of the men, and they were soon all rushing up the steps as fast as they could go. Every man knew it was a fool who didn't jump when Cudgel yelled.

As they came out of the club door, all looking the worse for wear, they fell in, two-by-two, in military style.

Purgy released the children from the wall ring and they formed a straight marching line again.

Pigleg grizzled: 'Get me a ride, if you will, Mr Cudgel. Me stump is already red raw in this heat, and we've a long way to go.'

'Aye, aye, Cap'n,' answered Cudgel, before whistling to a man on the other side of the square. The man immediately jumped up and took hold of two poles extending from a comfortable padded chair that rested on an axle between two wheels. He ran over to Pigleg, who climbed up and plonked himself down on the chair.

'Let's go then,' barked the captain, with a wave of his hook.

With that, they all began marching.

They marched through Acnalbasac City and out into the desert the other side.

'We're on the western edge of the Desert of Arahas,' said Mustafa, as they left the city limits.

They marched… and marched... and marched.

The sun got hotter… and hotter... and hotter.

Tizzie had no way of telling the time, but she thought it must have been three or more hours before they saw a lone building on the horizon. As they got closer, she thought it looked like an old desert fort with whitewashed walls. Closer still, she was able to read the creaking sign above the gates:

FORT ARAHAS

A huge red flag was hung on a long pole over the gates. As they passed underneath the flag, Tizzie looked up and studied it. There was a black symbol set in a white circle on the flag. It looked like a thick capital 'E'.

'The Evstika,' spat Hans. 'I hate it and all it stands for!'

'Shhhhh,' cautioned Jack. 'You'll get yourself in big trouble if you're not careful.'

'Hmphf, don't care anymore,' grumbled Hans. But he still took Jack's advice and fell silent.

Inside the fort, Purgy drew out the long chain from the rings in the neck irons, and the children were corralled together in a fenced area. The rusty metal had now rubbed Tizzie's skin so much that it was bleeding quite badly.

As she and Jack compared wounds, four men in black turbans and black djellabarobes came to guard the children. Each had a curved sword in his sash belt.

'Right, that's our work done for today,' said Pigleg. 'Time for a well earned rest, lads.'

With that, the pirates trudged wearily off to their beds, obviously very tired from their night of wild partying at the Casablanca Club.

FIFTY-EIGHT

The Sandland Slave School

The four black-robed guards first organised the children into two groups: girls on the left, boys on the right. Then they sorted them by height: smallest in the front row, tallest at the back.

With the midday sun rising to its full glare, the children were made to stand very still. They stood. And they stood. And they stood. Tizzie still hadn't had any water. She felt dizzy. What are we waiting for? she wondered.

One little girl in the front row fainted. The guards left her where she lay.

Tizzie glanced around. An 'E' flag flew on a tall flagpole inside the fort. A portrait of a very strange-looking person was painted high on the courtyard wall. A statue of the same person stood on four tall columns in the corners of the courtyard. Busts carved in a likeness of the man's head were placed at intervals along the battlements.

Tizzie had seen these same statues, busts, pictures, and flags all over Acnalbasac City, but had thought little of it. Now, seeing so many all in one place made her wonder what they meant.

As if hearing her thought, Hans spoke.

'Zey certainly like ze emperor here, don't zey. I've never seen so many emblems to Evile in one place. Zey...'

'Hey Mustafa, what do you know about Mafi and the slave school?' interrupted Jack, in an obvious attempt to avoid Hans saying anything he might regret.

Tizzie listened as Mustafa told all he knew.

'Mafi Mook is the richest slave trader in the whole of Sandland, probably the wurld. He has over eighty wives and more than two hundred children. As you have seen, Mafi is very ugly. And he smells of stale sweat. He has only got so many beautiful young wives because he buys them. His wives are all slaves, except for the head one, Mrs Mook. She runs the school with him. And she's in charge of all the domestic wives and the harem wives. And they say she's even fatter and uglier and nastier and crazier than her husband.'

'Two hundred children! Wow!' exclaimed little Lucy.

'Yes, and I've heard that the children are kept in terrible conditions, except Mrs Mook's two children, of course, who are spoilt brats. And...'

Mustafa suddenly stopped talking, and all the slavechildren went quiet.

Mafi Mook had appeared in the courtyard.

FIFTY-NINE

The Dune of Doom

'Welcome to the Sandland Slave School,' began Mafi Mook, as another small child fainted in the front row.

'Your master, Captain Pigleg, has kindly brought you here for a two-day intensive course in order that you may better yourselves. But it would be unreasonable of you to expect him to pay for you all to make yourselves more employable as slave workers. Therefore, every day, before and after school, you will work to pay for your own education.'

Tizzie looked at Jack. He shrugged, as if to show that he had no more idea than she did as to what was coming next.

'So, before we go any further, I want to bring something to your attention. This hill here – we like to call it, *The Dune of Doom* – is a punishment hill designed for the instilling of discipline into those who do not do as they are told; by making them run up and down it until they are ready to comply.'

Tizzie followed Mook's pointing finger to look at the hill of sand in the middle of the courtyard. You could hardly miss it she thought... it's taller than a house!

'The Dune is not finished,' continued Mook. 'It is only half its intended size, so we will need your help building it. Your work will be to take these buckets and spades through those gates, fill the buckets right to the top with desert sand, and bring them back here. You will then go to the top of The Dune and deposit the sand. You will do four hours of dune-building in the morning before school begins, and you will do four hours in the evenings, after lessons. There will be no food or drink – morning or evening – for *anyone* until you have *all* completed the dune-building to our satisfaction.'

Jack looked despairingly at Tizzie. 'The younger ones might not be able to do eight hours a day on that hill,' he whispered.

Mafi Mook spoke again. 'Which brings me to your schooling. First, we will sort you into groups, according to the job we think you are most suited to. Then we will give you instruction, to teach you to be good at those jobs.

'Most of you will learn the tasks well and pass your tests. If you succeed, your Master, Captain Pigleg, will be given a Slaveworker Certificate with your name on it.

'You will receive an iron wristbrace – stamped with the Slavemark of the Sandland School of Slaving – and so will be able to get good slave jobs for the rest of your life.

'So, that's the carrot, now for the stick…

'If you fail to complete the course satisfactorily, you will have no qualifications and will therefore be of little value as slave workers. Captain Pigleg informs me that those with the lowest marks will be *first* on Grunter's menu.'

Strangely, Mook ended his Welcome Speech with a comment that made it appear as if he thought he was doing everyone a big favour by allowing them to attend his institution.

'I wish each and every one of you good luck, and I hope you enjoy your short stay at the Sandland Slave School.

'And now… it's time for some dune-building practice.'

Two of the men in black turbans then opened the fortress gates as 'Mad Mafi' Mook concluded with an instruction…

'Pick up a bucket and spade on the way out.'

SIXTY

Laundry Girl

In the hours since Mafi Mook had finished his speech, Tizzie had climbed the Dune of Doom with a bucket full of desert sand more times than she could remember. She had sand everywhere – in her hair, in her eyes, in her mouth – and was now sitting exhausted in the slave pen on the floor of the sandy courtyard with the other children.

Men and women carrying clipboards, all dressed in the garb of Sandland, were walking over towards them.

'Here come the Slave Selectors,' said Mustafa. 'They're going to interview everyone and write down something called a Curriculum Vitae for each one of us.'

'It's called a CV for short,' added Jack. 'Make sure you tell them if you've already passed any exams at school or if you're good at anything like music or drawing or sport. The more you've got to offer, the less likely they are to give you nasty jobs.'

Tizzie watched as the children talked amongst themselves, trying to help each other remember everything they had done or were good at.

Jack turned and spoke in a low voice to Tizzie.

'I'm afraid I've heard that Mafi Mook has already decided on a nasty job for you, Tizzie… not much fun being a laundry wife.'

But then, as he saw Tizzie's head drop and he realised what he had said had upset her, he added something to make her feel better.

'Could be worse though; at least you didn't get the phosphate mines.'

Tizzie couldn't think of anything much worse than being a laundry wife, except, perhaps, being a meal for Grunter or shot by Blunder Bess.

All the children thought about what they had been good at in school, and most could remember which exams or tests they had passed.

'No point telling fibs,' said Jack, 'you'll only get found out. They sometimes test you again.'

All the children were interviewed, and things were written down on their CVs. Except Tizzie, who was taken, without an interview, straight to a room with a large sign above it: *Laundry*.

She was shoved through a door… straight into a wall of noise and heat and steam.

SIXTY-ONE

Dirty Smelly Nappies

A young woman walked out of the steam towards Tizzie. She was carrying what appeared to be a huge pile of dirty nappies, which she placed on a table.

Tizzie was pushed towards the table. Now she was sure they were nappies... because of the smell. Two hundred children, thought Tizzie; that's a lot of nappies.

'YOU, GIRL!' bawled a very large woman, whose whole body was covered from head to toe by a draping black cloth, 'come over here.'

Tizzie walked towards the woman.

'I am Mrs Mook! Wife Number One. I hear you might be the new laundry wife; number 83.'

'Yes,' said Tizzie.

'YES, MRS!' scowled Mrs Mook, as she slapped Tizzie hard across the face. I am *Mrs* Mook. The only Mrs!'

'Sorry... Yes Mrs,' whimpered Tizzie, her cheek still smarting from the slap.

'Pick up this pile of nappies and follow me. We're going to show you how to wash them properly.'

Tizzie picked up the pile of nappies. They smelt even worse so close to her nose. She hoped the laundry had some sort of washing machine.

However, it was soon clear that this was wishful thinking on her part. All the washing had to be done by hand. Tizzie was shown the stove, and instructed how to light it and heat the water and transfer the liquid to a washing tub. She was told to first scrape the bulk of the baby mess from the nappies into a hole in the ground called a 'poopit' behind the laundry. Then she had to wash off the worst of the soiling in the tub and discard the water. Then she had to heat more water and wash the nappies very thoroughly again with hard soap, using a scrubbing board. After that she had to run each nappy through a mangle and hang it out to dry in the sun. Finally, she had to iron and fold every nappy perfectly and stack them in the huge walk-in nappy cupboard in neat piles of ten.

Tizzie completed her target of one hundred nappies in the work shift and, by the end of it, was actually thinking that The Dune was nicer work. She couldn't imagine having to do this sort of slave work every single day for the rest of her life.

However, she had tried her hardest and was very pleased with the quality of her cleaning. All the nappies were spotless, with the exception of one that had been very badly stained to start with.

Even so, she was very pleased that she had managed to get the worst of the stain out with an hour or so of hard scrubbing.

At dusk, Mafi Mook came to inspect the nappies personally.

'Since you are to be my laundry wife – assuming you survive the trip to Jungleland and return to us in one piece – I'm taking a special interest in your work,' he smirked, as if he thought Tizzie should actually be pleased about the prospect of becoming 'Wife Number 83'.

'She's useless,' scowled Mrs Mook, holding up a nappy to her husband. 'Look, this one is still stained.'

'But it was already…'

'SHUT YOUR MOUTH, LAUNDRY GIRL,' screamed Mrs Mook, giving Tizzie another face-slap. 'I'M TALKING!'

'One not done properly,' mused Mafi, shaking his head as if it was a major failure.

Mrs Mook looked on triumphantly as her husband continued.

'That means only ninety-nine out of a hundred, I'm afraid,' he said, with an air of genuine disappointment about him.

But it's like getting 99 per cent, thought Tizzie indignantly, though not daring to speak up for herself again.

'That's only a B then,' concluded Mafi, still shaking his head as he entered the result in a box on his score sheet.

Tizzie had no way of knowing, but thought this *must* constitute a pass. Surely she wouldn't be first in line for being boar bait with that score.

After slave school, Tizzie joined the others for another four hours of dune-building. Once again, it was back-breaking work and she was absolutely exhausted when she finally got to lie down on the floor of a 'Female Sleeping Cell' at midnight.

The girls had been separated from the boys. There were supposed to be three cells for girls, but Purgy had thought it amusing to leave the neck irons on the girls, before making them cram into one cell, where there was only just enough room for each child to lie down on the floor.

Every time someone moved, the chains rattled and pulled, and those nearest to them on the chain were woken up.

As Tizzie sobbed to herself and tried to get to sleep for the third time, she just could not stop worrying about everything over and over again. Most of all she hoped that Louis had somehow survived and that she would one day be able to see him again.

SIXTY-TWO

Slave Marks

The slavechildren were called from their sleep just before dawn and brought into the courtyard for roll call.

Taking this brief opportunity to talk to the boys, Tizzie learned that Hans was going to be a slave-miner, the worst slave job imaginable. Although he had passed lots of exams at school, Hans had told the Slave Selectors that he didn't have any qualifications at all. So they'd taken one look at his muscles and put him down for the phosphate mines. He had been learning to crack rocks with something called a 'rockhammer'.

Jack had been a bit cleverer. He'd mentioned that he had some training as a magician and made it sound like it was 'magic tricks' rather than real magic training with Reddadom, the Red Wizard. So, he had been selected to be a Jester Slave – an entertainer to important people – which was apparently a bit of a soft option when it came to slavework. Jack had learned fire eating and sword swallowing on his first day.

Tizzie was a little bit envious that Jack was having fun whilst she was washing nappies. But she knew it wasn't Jack's fault.

At the end of the day, it was confirmed that Tizzie had earned an overall 'B' pass.

Some of the children had got an 'E'. All seven of them began sobbing at the thought of being first in line as bait for Big Red Grunter.

Tizzie felt very sorry for them.

But everyone felt most sorry for the one person who had got 'F' for 'Failed'. It was Hans, who said he'd done it on purpose.

'I didn't vant a certificate to vork in ze phosphate mines,' he complained. 'I don't care what Pigleg does to me. I don't care about anyzing anymore.'

Jack tried to placate his friend, but the muscular youth was inconsolable.

Later, after they had finished dune-building duties, Tizzie went along with all the others to the blacksmith's yard. Here, their wristirons were welded on. The solder was thick and strong. The thick iron bracelets were obviously intended to stay on forever.

Like all the others, Tizzie's wristiron was stamped with the slavemark from the Sandland Slave School. It took the form of a logo made up of three capital SSSs set close together, with a series of numbers after them; her unique identification for life. She studied the characters:

SSS 616333

Tizzie and Pritti compared their slavemarks.

SSS 616334

'If these are consecutive numbers, there have been a lot of slaves through here,' said Pritti. Tizzie agreed.

They then trudged back to the courtyard for the Leaving Ceremony, escorted by the silent guards with black turbans.

Prior to Mafi Mook's arrival, Pigleg said a few words, instructing them that they all had to say, 'Thank you', to the headmaster for giving them such a great opportunity to make something of themselves at the Sandland Slave School. The captain ended his short speech with: 'shukran' is the word for "thank you" in his language.'

All the children had to practise it.

'Shukran, Headmaster Mook.'

'Shukran, Headmaster Mook.'

'Shukran, Headmaster Mook.'

Tizzie joined in with all the others. She had decided that total compliance and obedience were the best ways to survive for now.

In flickering torchlight, the slavechildren were then lined up for a final roll call. Once again, the boys were on the right, and the girls on the left, tallest at the back, shortest at the front.

But, this time, when it came to calling the name of the broadest boy, there was silence.

Hans was missing.

SIXTY-THREE

Cheetahounds

A murmur went along the slave lines.

Everyone knew Hans had been feeling low. But to try to escape now, before they had thought of a plan, was stupid. And to run off into the desert… surely that was madness. The punishment would be terrible.

'He's been a captive for so long, I think it has driven him a bit crazy,' said Jack ruefully. 'And being selected for the phosphate mines was the straw that broke the camel's back.'

'If we lose a slave, we'll have to compensate,' screamed Headmaster Mook, glancing nervously at Captain Pigleg. 'Not to mention the damage to our reputation all over Erthwurld.'

He then barked urgent instructions to six of his henchmen.

'Find him… and find him quick!'

The six black-turbaned men ran out of the courtyard to another part of the fort. A short while later, they came back with twelve mutant animals straining on twelve long leads; two mutants to each man.

'Cheetahounds,' said Yang in awe. 'I've heard of them but never seen one before. They can track anything with their sense of smell, even in the desert. And they're the fastest land animals on the planet.'

The tracking animals each took a sniff of the spade that Hans had been using for dune-building.

'They're getting his scent,' informed Yang.

'He'll never get away with those beasts on his trail,' mourned Mustafa. 'And they'll tear him apart when they catch him.'

'*If* they catch him,' muttered Jack in an attempt at optimism, but it wasn't very convincing.

The pursuers had mounted their two quadcamels, with three men now sitting in the spaces between the four humps on each of the huge ships of the desert.

As she watched the cheetahounds and quadcamels chase off through the open gates in clouds of dry dust, Tizzie hoped and hoped Hans would get away.

'And don't come back without him,' yelled mad Mafi Mook after them.

'Dead or alive.'

SIXTY-FOUR

Caravan To Jungleland

The Great Simoom had been blowing for a week.

Like the desert riders, Louis had been confined to the tents at Camp Oasis. It was far too dangerous to go out in the sandstorm.

Then, as suddenly as it had started, the storm abated. Louis looked out of his tent to see a group of four desert riders leaving the camp, each on a camel laden with empty water bags.

Akbar was walking towards Louis' tent and spoke as he got closer: 'We will need fresh water for the journey to Jungleland. They are going to the Deep Well.'

Later that day, Louis was playing chess with Akbar when they heard a commotion outside. The inquisitive boy followed the sheik out of the tent.

There he saw two enormous camels, each with four humps.

Two of the desert riders held the reins of the camels as they sat behind the first humps. Between the next two humps on each of the camels were slumped the two other desert riders who had left that morning. They were covered in blood.

Behind the third hump on one of the huge camels was a youth with blond hair who appeared to be somewhat desert-worn. His skin was blistered and burned, and he had severely dried and cracked lips.

'When we got to the Deep Well, chasers from Fort Arahas had just caught this young man as he was drinking there,' said one of the riders to Akbar. 'They were beating him. We fought them and rescued him… and, as you see, we liberated their quadcamels too.'

Then the man turned and nodded at the two wounded men, saying simply: 'Cheetahounds.'

Akbar could see the men had been savaged badly. He clapped his hands.

'Quickly, tend to the wounded.'

The sheik then turned his attention to the blond-haired young man and helped him dismount from the quadcamel.

'Come, we will get you some food and water, and you can tell us how you came to be at the Deep Well… a fugitive of the slave traders. But first, introductions. I am Akbar, a Sheik of Sandland, what is your name?'

'Hans.'

Inside the tent, Louis listened as Hans told his story to Akbar Sharif.

When he got to the part where he mentioned 'Tizzie' – a little fair-haired girl they saved from the piranhasharks – Louis couldn't disguise his excitement.

'That's my sister!'

Akbar smiled warmly before asking Hans to continue. Louis felt very worried for Tizzie when Hans got to the part about Pigleg's plan to make her and the other children bait for Big Red Grunter or, if she survived, to sell her as a slave wife.

After Hans had finished telling them everything, Louis just had to ask a question of Akbar: 'Can we go to the fort and rescue Tizzie?'

Akbar shook his head.

'Unfortunately, that is impossible, my little warrior. The slavechildren only attend the school for a couple of days to get their Slaveworker Certificates and Slavemark Stamps. They will be long gone from there by now.'

Louis' head dropped, but he was cheered up enormously by what Akbar said next.

'However, we shall get on our way to Jungleland immediately. And, now that we have two quadcamels, we will be able to get there much more quickly.'

Camp Oasis was a hive of activity as the desert riders prepared the quadcamels for departure.

'I'm afraid that the fight with Mafi Mook's men means that my riders will have to stay behind to defend the camp, in case of a reprisal attack,' said Akbar to Louis.

'But I will keep my promise and take you to Nwotegroeg in Jungleland, and do what I can towards the rescue of your sister.'

'I vould like to come too,' said Hans. 'My friends are with Tizzie.'

'Of course,' agreed Akbar.

A short while later, they were ready to leave the camp.

They climbed on to their mounts, Akbar at the reins of one, and Hans the other. Louis sat behind Akbar, between the second and third humps of the quadcamel.

'We may have only two,' said Akbar with a smile, 'but we say in Sandland that "more than one camel is a caravan!"'

So it was that Louis, Hans, and Sheik Akbar Sharif, set off across the desert, travelling south in a camel caravan... destination Jungleland.

SIXTY-FIVE

Bound For Jungleland

During the night of Hans' escape, Tizzie didn't sleep much at all for worrying about what might happen to her friend.

Next morning, she got up early with all the others. After a breakfast of stale flatbread, chewy sheep's eyes, and sour, lumpy milk, they were lined up for one last roll call.

Mafi Mook waved goodbye to all the slavechildren as they left Fort Arahas and the Sandland Slave School.

As she shuffled past him with her chains on, he singled Tizzie out for a special comment: 'Goodbye for now, laundry girl. Hope to see you soon.'

The slave chain jangled along the road in sweltering heat. After the long march, they arrived back at the Port of Acnalbasac and the children were herded on to *The Revenger*.

Lying exhausted and badly sunburned in the hold, Tizzie reflected on her situation. Things didn't look good. She was a slave on a pirate ship bound for Jungleland... and she had no idea what had happened to her little brother or how she could possibly escape.

Her longer-term prospects were equally worrying.

Big Red Grunter.

Blunder Bess.

Mafi Mook.

Would she be eaten by a big pig, maimed by a thunder gun, or married for the rest of her life to a mad monster?

- NEXT -

After reading *Invasion of Evil*, the third book in the Kernowland series, you may want certain questions answered:

Will Tizzie be eaten by a big pig, maimed by a thunder gun, or married for the rest of her life to a mad monster?

Will Louis be able to reach Jungleland and rescue his sister?

What will Princess Kea, Mr Sand, Clevercloggs, and Misty find on the other side of the Crystal Door?

Who or what is coming to Kernowland in the Viking tentraft, and devouring whole reindeers on the way?

Can Megan the mermaid survive without her tail?

What will Cule Chegwidden do now?

What will it be like living in Kernowland under the cruel rule of Manaccan the Merciless?

Many other questions may have been raised in your mind.

If so, you may get some answers by reading *Book 4* in the Kernowland series:

Pigleg's Revenge

Visit our website for up-to-date information

www.kernowland.com